Movement from Hector c[illegible]tus' attention. Seeing the robot raise a hand in his direction, he dove to the floor as something like a cannon punched a hole through the back of the chair where he'd been sitting. (Apparently, although he had stopped Fokine from issuing whatever command he'd been intent on, in assaulting the man with his own desk Lotus had triggered the protection sequence in the robot.)

Acting on instinct, Lotus — reaching under the now-blasted chair — got a hand on its seat and then flung it towards Hector. As the robot caught the makeshift missile, Lotus scrambled towards the side of the desk. Bracing his back against it and pushing at an angle with his legs, he began lifting the huge desk up lengthwise. At the same time, he heard the sound of cloth ripping and wood splintering. He understood almost immediately what this meant: that Hector had torn the remnants of the chair apart.

Just as he got the desk up, the door to the office flew open and a trio of armed men stormed in. Although he couldn't see it on the other side of the desk, Lotus heard the cannon sound again, and one of the security guards flew backwards with a hole punched in his chest. Covered with gore, the two remaining guards beat a hasty retreat, barely escaping unscathed as Hector fired another shot that blasted a hole in the wall.

The robot then turned its attention back to Lotus…

The Chronos Ring Series
Eon (Chronos Ring #1)
Infinity (Chronos Ring #2)

INFINITY
Chronos Ring #2

By

Earl E. Hardman

INFINITY

Cover Design by Isikol

Edited by Faith Williams, The Atwater Group

This book is published by Vin-Vid Publishing.

ISBN: 978-1-937666-37-8

Printed in the U.S.A.

ACKNOWLEDGMENTS

I would like to thank the following for their help with this book: GOD, with whom all things are possible, and my family, which has continued to support my writing efforts.

INFINITY

Chapter 1

Grate Nicodemus, head of Galactic Intel, was sitting at his desk in his primary office on Terran IV when a message came through asking for an emergency meeting. The request was from Garrick Montale, Special Assistant to the High Council of the League of Planets.

Nicodemus sighed. Montale was the Council's lapdog — a minion more than happy to do whatever dirty work his masters asked of him. Frankly speaking, Nicodemus hated interacting with the man and had generally been able to avoid him by dealing directly with the Council on most matters. Occasionally, however, situations like that before him arose where it was clear that the request for a meeting came from the Council itself. That being the case, he could hardly refuse.

Taking another look, Nicodemus saw that the request was for an *immediate* emergency meeting. Grimacing (and despite the fact that it would require him putting other matters on hold), Nicodemus reluctantly accepted the request. Within seconds, two holograms appeared in his office.

The first was, of course, that of Montale. About average in terms of height and weight, he had dark-gray hair that gave the impression that he was entering early middle age. Although he didn't appear particularly imposing, he was a veteran of several military campaigns and was not one to underestimate in a fight. In addition, there was a hard edge to the man that seemed to come through even via hologram; it had made him unsuitable for civilian life, but he had apparently found his calling working — although mostly on unspecified assignments — at the highest levels of government.

The other person who appeared by hologram wasn't human. It was a tall, thin humanoid creature named Gourdatungazada (but who, thankfully, went by Gourd). He was the ambassador for his race, the Corsians, among humanity, and Nicodemus had worked closely with him in the past — quite recently, in fact. His presence at this meeting was unlikely to be a coincidence.

"I don't have a lot of time, Montale," Nicodemus began. "What's on the Council's mind?"

"Ian Lotus has escaped," Montale said matter-of-factly.

Nicodemus exchanged a quick glance with Gourd, and then asked, "Who's Ian Lotus?"

Montale laughed. "Do we really need to play games at this point? The Council is well aware of Ian Lotus, as you already know, and I represent their interests, which I'm sure you'd acknowledge."

There followed a few moments of tense silence, at which point Gourd spoke.

"Mr. Montale," said the Corsian ambassador. "A well-known tactic for procuring information from someone about a topic is to pretend to be familiar with the subject and then ask questions about it. Nicodemus did not reach his current position by being loose with information at his disposal."

Montale contemplated for a moment. "In other words, you want me to prove that I'm really in the know as opposed to simply being on a fishing expedition for information."

"Humor me," said Nicodemus.

"Very well," Montale said. A moment later, the image of a man — tall and well-muscled — appeared in Nicodemus' office. Young and handsome, the image's most striking feature was a wisp of white hair extending up from the center of his forehead into an otherwise all-dark head of hair.

"Ian Lotus," Montale continued, indicating the image. "Also known as Al Chronos. Also known as Gilgamesh. Believed to have other aliases which are — at present — unknown. He is confirmed to be over one hundred years old, but if his own claims of being born in the late twentieth century are true, he is considerably older."

"Let me jump in here for a second," Nicodemus interjected. "Giving you the benefit of the doubt, how's he lived so long?"

"The source of his longevity and continued youth is a mystery, but believed to be the result of having an alien father. However, it might also be related to an unusual pendant — a relic of some sort — that he wears around his neck and purportedly never takes off."

"What about his non-terrestrial parentage?" asked Gourd. "What more is known of that?"

Montale seemed to hesitate for a moment before replying, as if concentrating on how to phrase his response. "Our best information would seem to indicate that his father is some powerful, extra-dimensional being called Eon. He rules absolute in a separate continuum where he is apparently worshipped as a god. It was information from him that allowed Ian Lotus — under the alias of Al Chronos — to construct the Chronos Ring."

Of course, each of the three participants in this conversation knew what the Chronos Ring was: an expansive group of large metal orbs comprising an unimaginably colossal halo around the region of space inhabited by humans. It was the first and last line of defense with respect to protecting mankind from its enemies.

"In general," Montale continued, "the Chronos Ring functioned without issue for decades — since its construction, to be precise. But the Ring's controls were overridden quite recently, allowing several Parsnaak ships to enter human-occupied space."

"I'm aware of that," Nicodemus said. The Parsnaak were a vile race of reptilians — sworn enemies of mankind. "I'm also aware that the Ring was brought back online and the threat of Parsnaak invasion brought to a halt."

"Yes," Montale acknowledged. "Ian Lotus was involved in those events. In fact, he was wounded in the process of reactivating the Ring and was convalescing on an unnamed planet when he escaped."

"That is the second time you have used that word — 'escaped,'" Gourd noted. "Was this man a prisoner of some sort?"

"Not per se," said Montale. "But it was critical that he be detained for reasons of galactic security. In essence, it turns out that he is the only person with the access code that allows for command and control of the Chronos Ring."

"So, how did he 'escape,' as you put it?" Nicodemus asked.

Montale frowned. "We don't have all of the details at the moment, but he was on a world with just one port for space travel. With a single point of egress from the surface, it seemed unlikely that he could depart the planet without notice."

"So what happened?" asked Gourd.

"It appears that he somehow boosted the thrusters on an aircar significantly, getting the vehicle to catch up to a ship that was departing the planet. He then magnetically attached it to the ship an—"

"Wait," Nicodemus said, with a wave of his hand. "You're telling me that he accelerated enough to catch up to a ship that was leaving the surface?"

Montale nodded. "Yes. We estimate he was pulling between eight and ten Gs, at the very least. Probably more like twelve, to be honest."

"The average human tends to lose consciousness between four and six gravities," Gourd stated. "Are you certain he was conscious?"

"Without doubt," Montale said matter-of-factly. "For starters, it was an aircar, not a plane or a spaceship. It was designed to be driven by someone in conscious control. That aside, the movements of the vehicle — its flight trajectory, course corrections, and so on — all indicate that it was under the control of an alert and awake driver. We presume his ability to remain conscious is somehow tied to his unique physiology. He is reported to have prodigious strength and stamina."

"Any reason nobody blasted him out of the sky as he approached a ship that was leaving?" Nicodemus asked. "I would think that anything flying straight at a ship like that might be interpreted as an incoming missile."

"Two things," Montale said in reply. "First, that planet has been suffering from an odd anomaly recently with respect to its magnetic field. In short, the hulls of various ships have — for unknown reasons — become magnetized as they leave the surface, attracting various types of debris. Thus, the fact that something was flying at them was not completely a cause for concern."

"Still," Gourd observed, "I would suspect there is a notable difference between the odd piece of debris being attracted to a magnetized hull and something the size of an aircar."

"That would be the second thing," Montale announced. "Lotus somehow masked the signature of the vehicle such that it wasn't immediately detected by instruments either on the ship or the ground. Once in space, while the ship's crew went through procedures to de-magnetize the hull, he got to an airlock and gained entry."

"He opened an airlock from the outside?" Nicodemus asked, sounding impressed. "How'd he manage that trick?"

"He has what he describes as a low-level telekinetic ability," Montale responded. "That combined with a knowledge of the airlock design would allow him to open it and get inside."

"And then, when they jumped to hyperspace, he went with them," Nicodemus concluded.

"In a nutshell," Montale said.

"So what does the Council want with *me*?" Nicodemus asked.

Montale gave him a frank stare. "Assuming we're now past the point where you pretend you don't know who Ian Lotus is, the fact of the matter is that you knew him when he was Gilgamesh. More to the point, you were involved in the recent events related to the Ring's malfunction. Last but not least, that planet Lotus escaped from was one of the black op sites maintained by you as head of Galactic Intel."

"If it's one of *my* sites," Nicodemus retorted, "why is the Council getting involved? I'm perfectly capable of keeping my own house in order."

"Plainly speaking, Lotus is your friend — you and he go way back," Montale stated. "And, given his relationship with one of your operatives — your granddaughter, in fact — there's the possibility that suspicion may fall on you in relation to his escape."

Gourd made a sound of disdain. "You are operating at a disadvantage, and your implied accusations are without merit. You have facts related to Ian Lotus, but no real understanding of what they mean."

A bored expression latched onto Montale's face. "Please, enlighten me."

Gourd contemplated for a moment. "From your comments, you seem to be under the impression that Ian Lotus is, longevity aside, like most other men. If so, you are operating under a fallacy. Take the Chronos Ring, for example. As Al Chronos, he built it eight decades ago, and to this day, no other scientist has come close to even cracking its access code."

Montale shrugged. "So what's your point?"

"The point," Nicodemus chimed in, "is that almost a century ago, he was ahead of where our lead scientists are *today*. Technologically, we are way behind the curve in comparison to him."

"More to the point, there really is no comparison," Gourd added. "We're talking about a man who has had centuries, perhaps even millennia, to perfect every conceivable skill, talent, and ability — to gain in-depth knowledge of every discipline and specialty. Escaping from custody is probably child's play to him."

"And that's before you even get to the resources that such a man might have," Nicodemus said.

"What do you mean?" Montale asked, brow furrowed.

Nicodemus steepled his fingers, considering how to respond. "Imagine you could live for millennia. One day, on a whim, you establish a bank account with a single credit — maybe drawing interest of two-and-a-half percent annually. You come back a thousand years later. How much do you think that credit's grown to?"

Montale shrugged his shoulders. "I don't know. At two-and-a-half percent? Maybe a thousand credits?"

Nicodemus shook his head. "Too low. Try again."

"Ten thousand?" Montale suggested, only to see Nicodemus shake his head and point a finger upwards. "One hundred thousand? A million?"

"Try a billion," Nicodemus finally said.

"Actually, fifty-two billion," Gourd corrected.

Montale fought to keep his mouth from dropping open. "Are you saying this man is worth fifty-two billion credits?"

Nicodemus shook his head. "Not at all. Fifty-two billion is what he'd have if he put *one* credit in *one* bank with those terms for a thousand years. He could have significantly more if he deposited in excess of that or invested with a higher rate of return. Or significantly less, seeing as how we don't know his true age and he could very well be much younger than we suspect. I mean, if his money had far less time to grow, it might only be twenty billion total."

"The gist of all this," Gourd said, "is that it is a mistake to view Ian Lotus through the same lens you would use for other men. He is something far different."

Montale took a moment to absorb what he'd heard, and then stated, "All that aside, Nicodemus, the fact remains that Lotus probably counts you among his friends and he escaped from a planet over which you have ultimate jurisdiction. The Council is expecting you to present a plan for his recapture."

Without another word, Montale's hologram vanished. There was a silence for a moment, and then Gourd spoke.

"I'm going to assume that you already knew of Lotus' escape," the Corsian said.

"Of course," Nicodemus answered. "I'd be a terrible choice as head of intel if I didn't."

"Did you know he was going to make such an attempt when we left a week ago?"

Nicodemus pondered how to respond. Montale had been right in that both he and Gourd had been personally involved in the events relating to the repair of the Chronos Ring. Moreover, as the Corsian had just stated, they had both been with Lotus roughly a week earlier, leaving him to continue his recovery while they resumed the official duties of their respective positions.

"I suspected he might try to leave," Nicodemus finally said. "After all, he's a man who has managed to purposely maintain anonymity for quite some time. I'm sure he was quite uncomfortable having a lot of people — particularly people on the Council — learn who he was. At least he had the courtesy to wait until we left before he took off, so I can at least hold to the notion that it didn't happen on my watch."

"And now you assume he will try to vanish again. Disappear some place where people don't know him."

"Well, the man knows how to stay off our radar, blends in easily, and has no problem living a Spartan lifestyle. And the Council certainly didn't endear themselves to him, what with half of them seemingly obsessed with finding out the secret of his longevity, and continuously talking about him like he was a lab rat when he met with them."

"Your granddaughter — did she leave with him?"

"Monica?" Nicodemus said, and then shook his head. "No. What Lotus did in order to escape was incredibly risky — for instance, that aircar was practically shaken apart. It wasn't designed to be a rocket, and the remainder of it that was found floating in space was proof of that fact. My point, however, is that Lotus would never have risked Monica's life in that way."

"Are you curious as to how Montale knew so much of his background — his familial situation?"

"That was surprising. Only you, Monica, and I were with Lotus when he met his father, and I know that none of us talked about the experience."

"No," Gourd countered. "There was one other who learned the facts as we did."

"Hmmm," Nicodemus muttered, considering. "You may have a point."

"Lastly, what about Lotus'...companion?"

Nicodemus thought about this for a moment. What Gourd was referring to was a hulking, nigh-invulnerable colossus known as Cerulean — an Enforcer sent to Lotus from his extra-dimensional father as a gift...and protector.

Finally, Nicodemus let out a sigh and said, "If you're asking whether Cerulean could be the source of the Council's information about Lotus, I doubt it. His primary focus is protecting Lotus from danger. Besides, I've never heard the thing speak. To be honest, I'm not even sure it's alive in the way that you and I understand the word. If you're simply asking what happened to it, Lotus left it behind."

"Interesting…" Gourd said, obviously thinking. "Where is it now?"

"Still in the house where Lotus was residing before he left. It's not as if we can force it to move or anything. Our weapons don't have much effect on it — and threats? You might as well threaten a hurricane or a tsunami."

"So what are you going to do?"

Nicodemus shrugged. "About Lotus? I don't know at this point. Haven't decided what's in humanity's best interest yet."

Gourd smiled. "From any other person that would sound pompous or arrogant, but from you, it actually sounds sincere."

Chapter 2

Ian Lotus sat in a bar, sipping a locally made beer that was bitter beyond belief. As he imbibed, he realized that he was being made the butt of a joke: he had asked for something light and refreshing and had been served a mug of swill that was probably the chemical equivalent of tar.

This was not an unusual prank for people on various planets to play on outsiders. Some off-world tourist wants to sample some authentic local cuisine, so you serve him up the worst offal you can find and tell him it's a delicacy. *Ha-ha, so funny.* Well, Lotus refused to play along, instead choosing to wolf down the vile witch's brew they'd brought him like it was ambrosia, with an ear-to-ear smile on his face.

"How is it?" the bartender asked with a shifty smile on his face. He was a big, burly fellow who looked as though he also did double duty as a bouncer.

"Delicious," Lotus said, trying to sound sincere as he finished his drink. "I'll take another."

The bartender frowned, looking at Lotus as though his head was on backwards. He was obviously disappointed (as were other local patrons) that Lotus had not exhibited the anticipated reaction. Nevertheless, he puttered around behind the bar and brought forth another serving of the noxious brew a few minutes later.

On his part, Lotus barely noticed when a fresh mug had been placed in front of him. He had gone back to assessing his current situation and trying to determine his next move.

Escaping from that nameless, black ops planet had required a little ingenuity on his part — not to mention a certain appetite for risk. In addition to boosting the thrusters on an aircar well outside the vehicle's tolerances, he'd also had to don a makeshift spacesuit constructed from random odds and ends. Still, the riskiest part — not in terms of his life, but with respect to discovery — had occurred when he'd had to get to the airlock of the ship he'd hitched a ride on and get inside without being detected. (They had presumably chalked up the airlock opening to a systems malfunction.)

He had stealthily disembarked at the ship's first port of call, with the crew blissfully unaware that they'd ever had a stowaway. With some cash he'd managed to spirit away with him, he had immediately purchased a ticket on a cruise liner that was scheduled to make stops on ten different planets. Hoping to confuse any possible pursuit, he had gone planetside on the third world visited and simply foregone returning to the cruise ship. (He hadn't been particularly social or outgoing while on board, so it was unlikely that his absence would be noted right away — if at all.)

Of course, none of these hijinks and escapades would have been necessary if Cerulean, his erstwhile protector, had simply cooperated. The colossal Enforcer — a gift from Lotus' godlike father, Eon — had the ability to open a dimensional rift, thereby allowing for travel between disparate locations. Cerulean was supposed to be obedient to Lotus and subservient to his wishes. (In fact, the giant was supposed to be some sort of living extension of Lotus' will.) However — despite much pleading, cajoling, and demands — the Enforcer had not acted on Lotus' desire for a dimensional gateway off the black ops world. As a result, Lotus had been forced to come up with an alternative escape plan.

To be honest, however, the very thought that he might need protection was something of a novel concept for Lotus. He had survived this long without it. Of course, that had been before the recent discovery of his true paternity — and the existence of a younger half-brother, Nigel. As the elder of the two, Lotus was purportedly due to inherit all of their father's power one day. As a precursor to this, his father had deposited into Lotus' subconscious a vast amount of knowledge and memories. Unfortunately, his new half-brother didn't take too kindly to suddenly being bumped to second-in-line, and that fact alone had put Lotus' eventual death very high on Nigel's to-do list. And, now that he reflected on the resources previously at Nigel's disposal, maybe some type of protection was indeed warranted.

With that thought in mind, Lotus spent a moment wondering what would become of Cerulean. He'd hated leaving the Enforcer behind, but he had barely managed to finagle his own escape. Trying to do so with a hulking brute in tow would have been impossible.

Fortunately, there was little chance of anything untoward happening to Cerulean. Enforcers, from what Lotus had experienced, seemed to be immune to conventional forms of harm. Guns, grenades, etc., had little discernable or lasting effect on them. And even if the big guy had been susceptible to injury, Monica would be around to help him.

Now that she had come to mind, Lotus thought wistfully of his former lover. There was no way he would have risked her life the way he had his own in making his escape. Besides, she really didn't need to make a bolt for freedom as Lotus had; she was Nicodemus' granddaughter, and could surely come and go as she pleased. More to the point, she was also one of Nick's intelligence agents and — to be frank — although he cared deeply for her, Lotus still wasn't sure how much he could trust her. And so, like Cerulean, he had left her behind as well.

Lotus absentmindedly took a sip from the mug in front of him. The foul taste instantly brought him out of his reverie and back to the present. More specifically, it turned his focus back to the current problem of figuring out his next move, which had actually morphed into a two-fold dilemma.

First and foremost, he probably needed to leave the world he currently found himself on, a mostly-agricultural planet known as Oasis XII. The interplanetary government may have been a little slow on the uptake, but the people comprising it weren't stupid. It wouldn't be long before they tracked him down. He needed to be gone by then, but to make an effective disappearance he needed more cash than he currently had at his disposal.

Oddly enough, money in and of itself wasn't the problem. Lotus had various accounts all over the place with enough money in them to buy a solar system. The issue was access.

Now that people (that is, the government) knew about him — in particular, his longevity — they were aware of what to be watching for. Basically, most of his bank accounts were pretty old; that being the case, all they really had to do was just monitor aged accounts — particularly those that had been dormant for a while — for any type of activity.

It also didn't help that Lotus had been accompanied by Monica when he had recently accessed one such account. (Of course, that was before he knew she was a government agent.) The question was whether she had conveyed any of that info to her handlers (other than her grandfather, whom Lotus trusted to a certain extent), and if so, how much? And how old would an account have to be to trigger government interest? A hundred years old? Fifty years? Twenty?

Lotus leaned back in thought for a second, causing cold metal to touch his chest. It was the pendant that he always wore — which wouldn't, in fact, come off. It was some sort of heirloom from his father which, among other things, identified Lotus as Eonian royalty. That aside, he'd almost sell the thing if he could in order to get the funds he needed. Better that than to get caught and end up in an off-the-grid lab somewhere, with people taking him apart piece by piece in order to learn what made him tick.

Also, while the money situation was the major issue, it was only part of the problem, although the other part of Lotus' dilemma was more personal in nature.

Had anyone asked him, Lotus would probably have sworn that he had booked passage on the cruise liner without much notice to its ports of call and then disembarked on Oasis XII at random. Truth be told, however, he must have subconsciously noticed something, because this wasn't just a random world that he had ended up on. He had been here before. In fact, years earlier, he had lived on this particular planet.

In retrospect, Lotus could probably be forgiven for not immediately realizing that the cruise he had booked was going by one of his old stomping grounds. After all, there were probably hundreds of planets named "Oasis" in human-occupied space, and he had been chomping at the bit to put some distance between him and the first place his escape vehicle had landed. However, the truth hit him the minute he stepped off the ship; even though skylines and topography had changed, he suddenly — almost instinctively — knew where he was.

Given his druthers, Lotus probably never would have set foot on this particular Oasis again. Now that he was here, however, he felt an obligation weighing on him. A duty.

He sighed. He needed to go see someone.

Decision made, Lotus was about to get to his feet when he noticed someone entering the bar. The new patron was an older man — maybe sixty — but with the gait and build of someone maybe twenty years his junior. With a purposeful stride, he walked over to a table where three younger men, all perhaps in their mid-thirties, were drinking an orange concoction from a curved bottle.

Without a word, the older man picked up a nearby wooden chair and, holding it by the legs, smashed it across the head of one of the men at the table. The chair splintered upon impact, sending the man who'd been hit sprawling to the floor unconscious, and leaving the older man holding about a foot of table leg in his hand.

The other two men at the table came to their feet in alarm, and at that juncture Lotus saw that they were both armed, with laser guns holstered at their hips. Both seemed to go for their weapons at the same time. The older man, moving with a speed that was absolutely uncanny for a man of his years, hit one of the two in the throat with the table leg before the fellow had even gotten a grip on his gun; eyes bulging, his victim went down gasping for air and clutching at his throat.

The last man at the table actually cleared his weapon from the holster, only to have the older man bat it away with the table leg as he tried to aim. The old guy then conked the younger man on the forehead with his makeshift club, causing the man to fall to the ground, stunned. The older man then got on top of him and brained the younger man again. Lotus, racing over, caught the older man's club arm before he could hit the fellow a third time.

"All right," Lotus said. "That's enough."

The older man seemed to growl in his throat and looked at Lotus like he couldn't really see him. He tried to yank his arm free of Lotus' grip but couldn't manage it.

"I said that's enough, Duncan," Lotus almost shouted. "You've made your point, son."

The old guy blinked several times and then stared at Lotus, seeming to truly take note of him for the very first time. A look of incredulity came across his face and then he muttered, "Dad?"

Chapter 3

"It's a trick," said Collin Dreamborn, Duncan's son. "He's a clone, or pulling some type of body-morphing con."

"It's not a trick," Duncan countered. "Don't you think I'd know my own father?"

Collin snorted. "You mean *step*father, at best."

That much, at least, was true. Lotus had married Duncan's mother, a young widow, when Duncan was still a small child.

"Biology doesn't enter into this, as far as I'm concerned," Duncan retorted. "He's the man who raised me. He's the only father I've ever known."

"But he's not the same man," Collin insisted. "He *can't* be."

Lotus sighed internally as Duncan and Collin continued arguing, preferring to stay silent. They were currently in the great room of the Dreamborn family home, a place that Lotus remembered as a large-but-cozy residence, which Duncan had expanded over the decades into a sprawling manor.

In addition to Duncan and Collin, there were four other members of their immediate family present: Duncan's wife, Desiree; Collin's wife, Rayven; and the twin daughters of Duncan and Desiree, Lara and Lena.

Lotus hadn't wanted to come here — the house, that is. It would have been enough for him to have seen Duncan and then moved on. His presence was, as he'd feared it would be, disruptive. Duncan, however, following their impromptu reunion at the bar, had insisted on his stepfather coming to meet the rest of the family. He had reluctantly agreed, although in retrospect they probably should have clarified how Lotus was to be introduced.

Not one to mince words, Duncan had merely called the family together (all except for several grandchildren, who were currently in school), and then said, "This is DeLeon Dreamborn — my dad." The argument with Collin had commenced immediately thereafter.

Tired of listening to the squabble, Lotus slipped unobtrusively from the room, heading towards where he remembered the kitchen as being located. The layout had changed slightly from his recollection, but he ended up in the proper location without much trouble. Once there, he had the food and beverage dispenser supply him with a glass of water.

As he took a sip, he glanced out a nearby window, noting crops in the distance being tended to by automated machinery. The Dreamborn family had been farmers for generations, and when Lotus had married Duncan's widowed mother, he'd taken on not just the Dreamborn name but the family business as well. (He had long ago ceased being attached to monikers, having changed his own name numerous times over the years.) That said, farming these days — as had been the case for a while — was much more industrialized than it had been historically, with the result being that farmers were more like mechanics and computer engineers than tillers of the soil.

"It's changed quite a bit, hasn't it?" said a voice from behind him. Lotus turned to find Duncan's wife, Desiree, standing behind him. Lotus remembered her as a beautiful young lady with a gentle demeanor. The intervening years had been kind to her, as she was now a handsome middle-aged woman.

"Not so much," Lotus answered. "You guys appear to have rotated in different crops and upgraded the machinery, but for the most part it's still the same in a lot of ways. As are you — you're still as lovely as the day Duncan first introduced you to me and his mother."

She blushed a little at that. "I remember. I was quite the tomboy back then, showing up at the house here in dirty jeans and with my hair all wild." Taking a seat at the kitchen table, she motioned for Lotus to join her, which he did.

"Well, you certainly had a reputation for being a tomboy, but on that day, as I recall, you showed up in a blue summer dress and with your hair and nails neatly done. Duncan's mother even commented on how beautiful you looked."

The corners of her mouth tilted up slightly into a smile. "I suppose I must be misremembering. I'm getting along in years, you know."

"It doesn't matter. I'm just glad Duncan took my advice and married you."

Desiree's eyes suddenly twinkled. "Oh? So it's you I have to thank for my nuptials. My father never thought Duncan would have the stones to ask me, but he did. Now I see that it's because you told him to."

Lotus chuckled. "I didn't actually *tell* him to do it. I just told him that he was a fool if he didn't. Speaking of your father, how is he by the way? And your mother?"

"They're well. Still healthy and active, although they've turned over most of their farm operations to my brothers."

"So, does your dad still have that weird canine-feline hybrid as a pet, Kitty-Rex?"

Desiree laughed. "Heavens no! That thing was ancient when I was growing up. It died of old age when Collin was still in diapers. I haven't thought about Kitty-Rex in over thirty…"

She trailed off, staring at Lotus intently.

He smiled. "You're thinking it, aren't you? That it's me."

She harrumphed. "What I'm thinking is that I'd like to see the knife trick." She pointed towards a nearby knife rack.

"No problem," Lotus said with a grin, and then went to retrieve a blade from the rack.

He chose a long-bladed boning knife, which he twirled back and forth through his fingers like a pinwheel as he came back to the table. After taking his seat, he gripped the knife in both hands and bent the metal blade double. Like a showman, he then tapped the bent blade on the table to show that it was still fully metal. A moment later, he clutched the blade once again and straightened it back out before handing the knife to Desiree for inspection

"I'll be damned," she muttered, as she stared at the knife. "It really is you, Mr. Dreamborn."

"As I always told you, please drop the 'Mister,'" Lotus said. "Also, I go by Ian Lotus now." *Although probably not for much longer*, he added to himself.

She was silent for a moment, then asked, "So what happened to you?"

"You mean my appearance? Why I still look the same?"

She shook her head. "No, let's come back to that. I'm talking about when you left — what, forty years ago?"

Lotus nodded. That was about the right amount of time. "I went after them. The ones who killed Gwen."

Desiree nodded. Duncan's mother, Gwendolyn, had been visiting relatives on a distant planet when the passenger ship she was taking for the return voyage was attacked by pirates. All aboard were killed.

"My understanding is that you only went to retrieve her body, leaving Duncan here to run things," Desiree said. "But instead of returning with her, you shipped the body back and stayed. They told us that you went after the pirates and were presumably killed trying to get revenge."

"That was the official report, yes."

"And unofficially?"

"Unofficially, the universe soon found itself short one crew of buccaneers."

"So you found them?"

Lotus closed his eyes and nodded, the memories coming back to him: his clothes soaked in blood…men pleading for their lives as he slaughtered them without mercy…

"So, when it was all over, why didn't you come back?" Desiree asked.

"Two reasons," Lotus said. "First of all, as you can tell, I don't age."

A confounded expression crossed Desiree's face. "I don't understand. What does that have to do with anything?"

"Because time seems to stand still for me. That being the case, it's often difficult for people around me — people *close* to me — to move on. To move forward.

To progress. Take Duncan, for instance. Had I come back, we would have fallen into the same roles, with me being the parent and him being the child, even though, biologically, he would become older than me. In short, the people in my inner circle may begin to stagnate in terms of their development if I stay in one place too long."

"So, if Duncan was ever going to reach his full potential, coming back here wasn't an option."

"Exactly."

Desiree frowned in thought for a moment. "How long have you been like this? Ageless?"

"Since I reached my mid-twenties, which was" — Lotus paused to consider for a moment — "a long, long time ago."

"How did it happen?"

"I myself had no idea until very recently, but it's...complicated."

Desiree was silent for a moment as she considered this. "Did Duncan's mother know? That you would stay young while she grew old?"

"Of course. I told her before we were married, which was the only proper thing to do. Still, I'm not sure she believed me. In fact, I was certain she'd consider me insane and call the whole thing off, which was something that had happened before."

Desiree ignored the implications of Lotus' last statement. "But she went through with it — marrying a guy who might be crazy."

"You have to understand that, possible insanity aside, we were soulmates. Each of us was one-half of a greater whole. I was just drifting from place to place at the time, unsure of what to do with myself next, when I found myself here on Oasis. She'd been in need of help with the farm since the death of Duncan's biological father; I was in need of something to give me focus and direction, and coming to work on the Dreamborn farm seemed to do that. Almost immediately, however, Gwen and I were drawn to each other in a fierce and intense way that defied explanation. We simply had to be together. As Gwen later put it, I could have been a cannibal and she still would have felt compelled to marry me."

Desiree snickered a little at that. "So she ignored the crazy talk and became your wife."

"Yes, and over time, she came to see that I hadn't been lying. Duncan was about five when we married and just entering his twenties when I left. In all that time, I never aged a day. People were starting to assume that Gwen was a mother of two instead of having a husband and a son."

"Did Duncan know about you?"

"He certainly noticed that I'd never gotten any older — especially with people constantly asking if we were brothers in the later years. I didn't find out until today, however, that his mother actually told him the truth about me before she left on that final trip."

In truth, it was one of many things Lotus and Duncan had discussed and caught up on while driving from the bar to the family farm.

Desiree merely nodded. "I suppose that explains why all of this is so easy for him to accept."

"I don't know if 'easy' is the appropriate term, but he's certainly had a lot of time to think about it."

"Okay," Desiree said with a nod. "So what's the other thing?"

Lotus looked perplexed. "Excuse me?"

"You said there were two reasons why you didn't come back. One was your immortality. What was the other?"

Lotus went silent, contemplating how to answer, and then let out a long-held breath. "I thought killing the pirates who murdered Gwen would satiate me, that serving justice on her killers — getting revenge — would ease the pain of losing her. It didn't. In all honesty, it lit some kind of fire in me, a bloodlust that I couldn't control. From that point forward, I was consumed with the thought of hunting down criminals like the ones who killed my wife and making them pay."

"So what did you do?"

"I changed my name and signed up for a patrol unit, one created to respond to the types of threats that had taken Gwen from me."

"So you hunted pirates."

"For a couple of years. During that time, nothing satisfied me as much as blasting those animals to atoms, sticking a blade in them, or just beating them down with my bare hands… And then one day, the craving was gone. I just woke up one morning and knew I didn't want to kill any more. I was just so weary of it all. So I resigned from my unit and moved on."

"And now you've come full circle, ending up back on Oasis where you started."

"So to speak. I'm not staying, though. In fact, I had a serious internal debate on whether to even seek out Duncan. Of course, that was before I saw him beating the stuffing out of three guys in a bar."

"Did he tell you what that was about?"

Lotus nodded. It was one of the things he and Duncan had discussed during their ride. "Kyzellium. You've got large plots of land filled with it."

"Yes," Desiree said softly. "It's funny. For years people on this planet threw that crap away, thinking it was a worthless mineral that interfered with planting. Now it's being hailed as a new power source and worth ten times its weight in gold. Some people around here are upset because they sold their mineral rights before the news really became public."

"But you guys didn't."

She shook her head. "No. We got offers, and the fact that the numbers were so off-the-charts should have told us something, but we just thought we were dealing with crazy off-worlders with more money than sense. If it had been up to me, I would have sold, but Duncan wouldn't even entertain the thought. Can you guess why?"

Lotus looked away for a second, almost embarrassed. "Because I told him not to."

"Exactly. He said that when he was growing up, you told him lots of times never to sell any of the mineral rights — especially to the kyzellium, because it would be incredibly valuable one day."

"It was just a guess," Lotus said with a shrug.

"Hmmm," she said with a frown. "Seems more like you knew, and it just took science a few decades to catch up with you."

"Anyway," Lotus said, ignoring her comment, "give me your take on this 'syndicate.'"

Desiree's face took on an odd expression, one that mingled multiple emotions at once: anger, fear, frustration, and more.

"I'm sure Duncan filled you in," she said after a moment. "They call themselves a corporation, but they're nothing more than thugs in suits. They've been forcing people around here to sell to them through intimidation and threats. There are even a couple of stories of kidnapping and torture."

"According to Duncan, they recently started coming after you guys."

"That's right. It was just little things at first. New equipment would stop working. Tools would come up missing. Alarms would start going off around the property at night. Just minor nuisances, to be honest."

"And then it escalated."

"Yes," Desiree confirmed. "Our vehicles started getting vandalized. Fires would break out in the fields for no apparent reason. We started getting anonymous, threatening notes telling us we needed not just to sell our mineral rights, but to leave Oasis. And then, yesterday, some men in armored vehicles surrounded our granddaughter's aircar as she was coming home from school with a couple of her younger cousins — the children of our twin girls — forcing her to stop."

"Duncan said she's okay."

"Yes," Desiree agreed. "She's tough, that one. Collin's girl. She's only sixteen, but she has a rod of steel in her and won't back down from anybody."

"So I've heard," Lotus said with a chuckle. "The way Duncan tells it, she got out of the car screaming obscenities."

"That's what her cousins said," Desiree acknowledged, smiling. "The men basically tried to scare her by telling her all the bad things that could happen to a young girl — the things bad men could do to someone like her. She wasn't frightened, but when Duncan heard about it... Well, you know the rest."

"Yes. He did his best to see how close he could come to killing three guys without actually crossing the line."

"I did what you would have done forty years ago, Dad," said a voice from the entry to the kitchen. Lotus turned and saw Duncan standing there. Behind him were Collin and the others. Duncan stepped into the room and took a seat at the table next to his wife. The others followed his example and also sat.

"Well," Lotus asked. "Did you decide whether or not I was telling the truth?"

"I don't need to decide," Duncan said. "I *know* it's you."

"Thanks, Dunc," Lotus said, noting that his stepson smiled at being called by his old nickname. "Why do I feel that there's a 'but,' coming, though?"

"*But*," Duncan said, meeting Lotus' expectations, "a couple of the others" — he gestured towards his children and daughter-in-law — "feel that, whether it's really you or not, it seems more than simply fortuitous that you happen to show up right when it turns out that our mineral holdings are likely to be worth billions."

Unable to contain himself, Lotus burst out laughing. The complete absurdity of what was being suggested was hilarious. *If they only knew...*

The others looked at him somewhat suspiciously, unable to figure out what exactly was so funny. After a few moments, Lotus was finally able to regain his composure.

"Let me guess," Lotus said, voice still full of mirth. "Collin's the skeptic."

"Well, my daughter-in-law is also supporting her husband's point of view," Duncan said. "The twins are deferring judgment for now, and as for their husbands, they're both off-planet at the moment, so we haven't solicited their opinions."

Lotus nodded, understanding that this last statement was a concession to him and his concern (previously expressed to Duncan) about off-world communications being monitored.

"Bottom line," Collin chimed in, "is that we think you want something. Even if my father's right about you being DeLeon Dreamborn — and I'm willing to give him the benefit of the doubt — I'm still not convinced that your sudden appearance is mere coincidence."

"Well, you're actually both right *and* wrong," Lotus said. "It *is* more coincidence than anything else that I happened to turn up here on Oasis. That said, I could indeed use your help with something, but I won't ask you to do it for nothing."

Collin frowned. "I'm not sure I understand."

"If you'll permit me," Lotus said, glancing around the table and looking at everyone in turn, "I'd like to make a proposal."

Chapter 4

"So, do we have a deal?" Lotus asked.

There was silence at the table, even from Duncan (whom Lotus was counting on for support). It had only taken him a minute to outline his proposal, which was actually pretty straightforward.

"I think we're fine with what you've proposed," Duncan said after a moment, causing Lotus to feel unexpected relief.

"Hold up," Collin interjected. "Maybe I'm misunderstanding something here, so let me just make sure I've got the facts right." He looked squarely at Lotus. "You claim you have a significant amount of cash at your disposal. However, for reasons you prefer not to disclose, you personally can't access it. So you want us to essentially give you what can't be called an insignificant sum of money, and in exchange you'll give us access to the account where you allegedly have these funds deposited. Do I have it right so far?"

"Pretty much," Lotus acknowledged. "Except my account will also contain enough money to cover interest for the funds you provide to me."

"Yes, the interest — can't forget *that*," Collin almost sneered. "Anyway, you'll give us access to the account, but we aren't allowed to do anything with it, including confirm what's in it, until you leave the planet."

Lotus nodded. "I think that essentially sums it all up."

Collin simply stared at him for a moment, then turned to his father and said, "Pop, if you give him a single credit, then you are the stupidest man—"

"DeLeon Collin Dreamborn!" his mother exclaimed, cutting him off.

"Enough!" Duncan roared at the same time, coming to his feet. "Don't forget who's the parent and who's the child here! It's *my* money, and if I want to piss on it, plant it in the soil, and try to make it grow into a money tree, then that's what I'll damned well do. Understand?"

Although he was clearly smoldering, Collin muttered a barely-audible "Yes, sir," under his breath.

Duncan sat back down, obviously miffed at his son. Silence reigned for a few uncomfortable seconds as an almost palpable tension filled the air.

Seeking to ease the growing strain, Lotus turned to Collin. "So, you're named after me?"

"What?" Collin asked, caught unprepared by the question.

"Your mother called you DeLeon a moment ago," Lotus stated. "Which I take it means you were named after me."

"I was named after my dad's stepfather, if that's what you mean."

"He was born just a year or two after you left," Duncan chimed in. "Somewhere along the way, we started calling him by his middle name, Collin, and it just stuck."

"Well, they're both fine names as far as I'm concerned," Lotus said.

"I'm so happy you approve," Collin mumbled sarcastically.

Suddenly angry, Duncan let out a harsh breath and was on the verge of saying something when a subtle gesture from Lotus made him stop.

Lotus gave Collin a very frank stare. "Look, I can understand your distrust, and on the surface, it certainly does have the appearance of being a con — and not even an elaborate one, at that. But I promise you, everything I'm telling you is true."

"That's easy enough to *say*," Collin noted.

"Unfortunately, I can't provide you with any proof that I'm being sincere. You won't have that until after I'm gone and you access the account."

Collin crossed his arms defiantly. "How convenient."

Lotus scratched his chin in thought for a moment. "Okay, in addition to the account I'm leaving, how about I sweeten the pot by offering something tangible that you can put a measureable value on?"

Collin leaned forward, interested in spite of his misgivings.

"I'll take care of your problem with this syndicate that's been harassing you."

There was silence for a moment, and then Collin nodded in agreement.

Chapter 5

Getting in to see Hari Fokine, head of the Zinnom Syndicate's operations on Oasis, took far more time than Lotus would have imagined. He had been advised to show up two hours early for his appointment, and, upon arrival, had immediately been subjected to what could only be described as extreme security measures.

First, he was made to strip out of the clothes he had worn for the meeting — a formal jacket, shirt, and dress pants — and required to don a simple, pocketless one-piece bodysuit. (His clothes, which were undoubtedly being searched, would allegedly be returned to him after his meeting with Fokine.) All that he was allowed to keep was his pendant, which he adamantly refused to take off.

He was then paraded through several scanners (as well as physically examined) until members of Zinnom's security detail were satisfied that he had no weapons secreted on his person. At that point, he was taken to a waiting room, where he sat around for an hour twiddling his thumbs until a couple of security guards arrived with news that Fokine was ready to see him.

Zinnom's corporate residence on Oasis was a high-rise office building located in Spring, the largest city on the planet. With the security guards serving as escort, Lotus was taken up by express elevator to the ninety-second floor, where Fokine's office was located. Once there, he was marched to a set of heavy wooden doors, where two other security guards were on duty. One of them opened the doors and motioned for Lotus to enter.

Inside, Lotus found himself in an oversized office that struck him as having an unusual layout. There was an area with a small but elegant dining table near a kitchenette. Not far away was a sitting area consisting of a ritzy sofa and several fancy lounge chairs, all arranged in front of an upscale vid-screen on one of the walls. Near the center of the room was a high-end holo-game table — an expensive toy capable of playing hundreds (if not thousands) of different games and offering various forms of entertainment. A door set in one of the walls presumably led to a washroom. Overpriced paintings hung on the walls, and there were even life-sized statues in a couple of art niches.

All in all, the room gave Lotus the impression of a place that probably served not only as an office, but also living quarters. (Moreover, the décor left him convinced that whoever officed here probably had more money than taste.)

The outer wall of the office, which consisted of a wall-to-wall picture window looking out over the city, was tinted to keep out the heat of the midday sun, but still allowed more-than-adequate light into the room. About a dozen paces away from the window was a large ornate desk, behind which sat a man whom Lotus assumed to be Fokine. With nowhere else to go, Lotus began walking towards him.

Behind Fokine and a little to his right was a figure that Lotus initially assumed to be another statue. However, as he drew closer, he saw that it was actually a robot. Over seven feet tall, the thing was heavily armored, with a darkened, bulletproof faceplate, reinforced metal on every inch of its exterior, and even pauldrons on its shoulders that arched down over the upper part of its arms. It swiveled its head slightly as Lotus approached, making sure he knew it was aware of his presence.

In addition to the robot, Lotus took the opportunity to size up Fokine as he walked towards the desk. The man appeared to be in his late thirties, with blue eyes and dark hair. He was about medium height and would likely be considered handsome by most women, but he exuded a certain smugness that probably detracted from his appeal.

There were two high-back chairs in front of the desk, and — rather than shake Lotus' hand when he drew near — Fokine merely motioned for his visitor to sit. Lotus took the proffered seat and flopped down.

"So, who's your friend?" Lotus asked without preamble, indicating the robot.

Fokine smiled. "This is Hector, from Stalwart Robotics' Guardian line, version seven point three."

"Stalwart, huh? I hear their robot protection units are the best you can buy."

Beaming at the opportunity to brag, Fokine said, "They better be, based on what this thing cost me. But Stalwart has been the gold standard for over two hundred years, and I wanted the best."

Lotus gave him a direct stare. "So what business does Zinnom engage in that requires its executives to need that type of protection?"

There was silence for a moment, and then — ignoring the question, Fokine said, "I don't have a lot of time, so let's talk about why you're here. I understand you're representing the Dreamborns, and you've come to make a deal to sell their mineral rights."

"Not exactly," Lotus clarified. "I'm here to make a deal, but not to sell you anything."

"Oh?" Fokine said, raising an eyebrow. "Then what deal are you proposing?"

"That you leave the Dreamborns alone — no more harassment, no more intimidation, no more threats. Do that, and things don't have to escalate."

Fokine frowned for a second, then let out a harsh bark of laughter. "You… You're threatening *me*? That's got to be the best joke I've heard all day!"

"It's not a joke, and it's not a threat. It's a guarantee."

Suddenly angry, Fokine leaned across the desk. "Let me tell you something. Nobody threatens Zinnom or any of our people. *We* make the threats. And we carry them out. So you can go back to your friends the Dreamborns and tell them that they can either sell to us, or things will 'escalate,' as you put it, in a major way. And trust me, they won't like the way it ends — those of them that survive, that is. Understand?"

"I understand," Lotus said with a nod, "but let me put my deal in very basic terms so that I make sure *you* understand." He leaned forward and put his hands on the edge of the desk. "Either leave the Dreamborns alone, or I…will…kill…you."

Fokine blinked, not seeming to understand what Lotus had said. "What?"

"Leave the Dreamborns in peace, or I'll ki—"

"Hector!" Fokine screamed. "Gamma nine beta — uhhff!"

Fokine didn't get to finish what Lotus assumed was a kill command of some sort. (Probably an order to eliminate everyone in the room except Fokine.) Immediately realizing what was going on, Lotus — his hands still on its edge — had given the desk a forceful shove. It had rammed into Fokine, knocking him over backwards and out of his seat.

Movement from Hector caught Lotus' attention. Seeing the robot raise a hand in his direction, he dove to the floor as something like a cannon punched a hole through the back of the chair where he'd been sitting. (Apparently, although he had stopped Fokine from issuing whatever command he'd been intent on, in assaulting the man with his own desk Lotus had triggered the protection sequence in the robot.)

Acting on instinct, Lotus — reaching under the now-blasted chair — got a hand on its seat and then flung it towards Hector. As the robot caught the makeshift missile, Lotus scrambled towards the side of the desk. Bracing his back against it and pushing at an angle with his legs, he began lifting the huge desk up lengthwise. At the same time, he heard the sound of cloth ripping and wood splintering. He understood almost immediately what this meant: that Hector had torn the remnants of the chair apart.

Just as he got the desk up, the door to the office flew open and a trio of armed men stormed in. Although he couldn't see it on the other side of the desk, Lotus heard the cannon sound again, and one of the security guards flew backwards with a hole punched in his chest. Covered with gore, the two remaining guards beat a hasty retreat, barely escaping unscathed as Hector fired another shot that blasted a hole in the wall.

A noise near his feet made Lotus look down. There, he saw Fokine still on the floor, retrieving a gun from one of the upturned desk's drawers. Before Fokine could point the weapon, Lotus stomped down hard on the wrist of the man's gun hand. He was rewarded with both a satisfying crunch of broken bone and a high-pitched scream from Fokine. Lotus kicked him squarely on the chin; Fokine's head snapped to the side, and he flopped to the ground, moaning.

The sound of a large body in motion put Lotus' focus back on Hector. The robot was moving around the desk in an attempt to get at him. For a second, he wondered why it didn't just start shooting through the desk, and then he remembered that Fokine was next to him. Being unable to see the two men, it couldn't fire without risk of hitting its charge.

Sensing the direction that Hector was moving in, Lotus stealthily circled around the desk and came up behind the robot. Before it realized he was there, he leaped onto its back. Reaching towards its left shoulder, he gripped the pauldron and yanked upwards, ripping it off.

Hector's arms came towards Lotus as the robot tried to reach up over its shoulder and grab him. As its left hand came up, Lotus grabbed it by the wrist and pulled as hard as he could. There was a muffled popping sound from somewhere inside the robot, and its left arm seemed to freeze in place, pointed upwards.

Grabbing the right pauldron, Lotus slid down Hector's back, tearing the piece of armor off as he'd done on the left as the robot reached for him. He then swiftly circled around under Hector's upraised right arm and pushed up on it. There was another muffled popping sound, and now Hector had both arms raised as though being mugged by someone with a gun. It whirled angrily in a circle for a few seconds, with blasts from its upraised hands punching holes in the ceiling and causing plaster to come down. Then, without warning, it stopped moving, stopped firing, and seemed to simply shut down.

"W-w-what did you do?" said a nearby voice that sounded particularly strained.

Lotus turned and saw Fokine standing by the desk, holding the gun he'd had earlier in his good hand while cradling the injured one to his chest.

"My robot," Fokine said, taking aim squarely at Lotus's chest. "What did you do to it?"

Lotus spent a moment contemplating his options. He was probably too close for Fokine to miss if he decided to shoot, but too far away to have a real chance of disarming the man. The logical alternative, then, was to stall for time — which in this instance meant answering the man's questions.

"There's a design flaw in this model," Lotus said, speaking truthfully. "There's a hinge in the shoulder that has a tendency to lock if the arm is raised too high. I'm assuming they didn't put that in the brochure." Fokine merely grunted in response, so Lotus went on. "Anyway, that's why it had this" — he raised Hector's right pauldron, which he still held — "on its shoulders. You probably thought it was just armor, but it was really intended to keep the robot's arm from going too high."

"How'd you shut it down?" Fokine asked. Obviously, despite his various injuries (including an ugly bruise that was forming on his chin where he'd been kicked), the man was concerned about the financial investment he'd made in the robot.

"Even with its arm locked in an upright position, the robot will still try to fire its weapons," Lotus said. "This can result in unexpected damage to both property and people, so there's an automatic shutdown procedure that's triggered if the hinge malfunctions."

Fokine gave him a dubious look. "And just how do you know all this?"

"I was involved in the design of Stalwart's original product line."

"The original..." Fokine mumbled, looking confused. Given that Stalwart was a company that was two hundred years old, Lotus' statement was plainly bewildering. However, before he could comment further, the office door burst open and this time half a dozen guards came in, weapons drawn.

Taking advantage of the distraction caused by the new arrivals, Lotus flicked his wrist, flinging the pauldron towards Fokine and then diving for cover just as the man fired. The side of the armor piece, torn and jagged where it had been ripped from Hector, sank deep into the shoulder of Fokine's good arm. Fokine screamed, then let the gun drop from his loose fingers.

The guards, already on edge and perhaps not realizing that Hector was shut down, reacted to the gunfire by discharging their own weapons. Lotus stared at the gun Fokine had dropped, concentrating; a moment later, it flew into his hand — a result of his telekinesis. Then, risking exposure, he took refuge behind the deactivated robot. Now burdened with yet another injury, a pale and shaken Fokine slumped to the floor behind the desk.

From his spot behind the robot, Lotus began to return the guards' fire. Zinnom's security detail had obviously received little in the way of training, because they stayed clustered together, apparently believing there was safety in numbers. The truth, however, was that, collectively, they formed a pretty big target. Lotus didn't even have to take aim, in all honesty; he just fired towards the mob of guards, and two of them went down almost immediately. Two of their colleagues abandoned the firefight in order to drag their injured comrades out of the room and to safety. Thus, only two guards remained.

Behind him, Lotus heard the window starting to crack. It was obviously made of some type of reinforced or bulletproof glass, but it had been under tremendous assault for the past few minutes. Moreover, it would probably only be a few moments before the remaining guards realized that all they were facing was one guy with a pissant little handgun. Then — or maybe when they got reinforcements (which were surely on the way) — they'd begin trying to outflank him. Assuming they didn't just end this thing by tossing a grenade in his direction.

Hmmm… That's not a bad idea, Lotus thought. It was risky, but he'd been pushing his luck since he'd first set foot in this office — since he'd first escaped that black ops planet, to be honest.

Tucking the gun under his arm, Lotus made a quick dash over to the desk and wrenched the pauldron out of Fokine's shoulder, who yelped in pain. Ignoring the blood on it, he then squeezed the piece of armor, compressing it into something like a metal ball.

Somewhat satisfied with his creation, Lotus glanced from behind the cover of the desk to get a bead on his trajectory. A moment later, he tossed the metal ball towards the two guards, at the same time yelling, "Grenade!" as loud as he could.

Peeking around the edge of the desk, Lotus saw the guards scramble wildly for the exit and then slam the door behind them. Not wasting a moment, he lifted the heavy desk en masse, raising it over his head, and then raced towards the double doors. Once there, he slammed the desk down, effectively blocking the entry.

Relief flooded through Lotus, but only for a moment as he suddenly realized something.

The gun!

He reached under his arm, but of course it wasn't there. It must have fallen out when he'd picked up the desk. That meant…

Slightly alarmed, he looked towards Fokine, expecting to see the gun trained on him. It wasn't. In fact, Fokine wasn't even sitting up. Without the desk to prop him up, the man now lay prone on the floor.

Approaching swiftly but warily, Lotus was relieved to see the gun lying on the floor where it had apparently fallen. Fokine, although practically within arm's reach of the weapon, hadn't made any attempt to claim it. In fact, with his clothes soaked with blood in the area where the pauldron had struck, Fokine looked like he might be going into shock.

After retrieving the gun, Lotus grabbed a fistful of Fokine's shirt near the man's neck and hauled him up. Lotus propped the Zinnom exec up against the window and shook him.

"Fokine!" Lotus shouted, shaking the man. "Fokine!"

Slowly, whimpering in pain, Fokine seemed to come back to himself.

"Where's your emergency exit?" Lotus asked forcefully.

"Wh-wh-what?" Fokine mumbled.

"Your emergency exit. Where is it?"

Fokine shook his head. "I don't…I don't have—"

"Cut the shit!" Lotus bellowed, shaking him again. "I've known plenty of wormy little execs like you, and they always leave themselves a back door — especially if they've also gone through the trouble of buying a Guardian 'bot for protection."

"All right, all right!" Fokine screeched through clenched teeth. "I'll show you."

****

The door in one of the office walls that Lotus had noticed earlier turned out to lead to a bedroom suite. In the bedroom itself, one of the paneled walls was actually the doorway to a hidden private elevator. The elevator, in turn, went down to a sub-basement level that served as a concealed garage space.

All of this was revealed by Fokine, who found himself being dragged along by Lotus as an insurance policy of sorts against anything untoward happening. Once in the garage (where three expensive-looking vehicles were parked), Lotus finally released his grip on Fokine, who slumped down onto his haunches. Having the garage wall to lean against seemed to be the only thing keeping the man from flopping completely onto the ground. Lotus bent down and looked him in the eye.

"Can you hear me?" Lotus asked. Fokine nodded weakly, and Lotus continued. "Good. Now, maybe not today, maybe not tomorrow, but at some point in the near future, everything that happened here today is going to seem like a bad dream. Probably at a juncture when your wounds are on the mend and you're once again surrounded by a security detail and a protective 'bot, you're going to look back on all this and think that it couldn't have been as bad as you remember. Then you're going to think about how someone came into *your* house and attacked you. It's going to make you upset. Then you're going to get angry. Then you're going to be looking to send a message that nobody does that kind of thing to you and gets away with it. In simple terms, you're going to be looking to get revenge. Let me tell you, that would be a fatal mistake."

Lotus paused for a moment, making sure that Fokine was actively listening before continuing.

"First of all, think about how things went down here today. I came to you, announcing my presence in advance. I waltzed into your office completely unarmed, practically naked in this stupid bodysuit. You had protection all around you. And despite all that, I was still able to turn the situation to my advantage, so that here I stand without a mark on me, while you're sitting there bleeding all over the place like you're being paid for it. However, if you do something stupid — like come after me or the Dreamborns — I can't promise this kind of happy ending next time.

"Basically, if we have to meet again, you won't see me coming, you won't get any warning, and I'll be armed to the teeth. Trust me, you don't want to see what I'm capable of with a full complement of weapons at my disposal. It will not go well for you." Lotus leaned in close. "Now, do we understand each other?"

Fokine nodded in response. Satisfied that the man was being sincere (at least for the moment), Lotus stood up and turned, assessing the vehicles parked in the garage. He chose the largest of the three, an oversized utility vehicle that seemed to be well-armored. He spent a moment hot-wiring the ignition and disabling the security features, including the GPS. (In retrospect, he could have gotten the starter sequence and passcode for the security options from Fokine, but it was almost faster — and a lot more fun — to circumvent the need for those things in criminal fashion.)

Now ready to depart, Lotus turned to Fokine one last time, noting that the man was staring at him with an expression that seemed to be an odd mingling of both anxiety and relief.

"I'm sure your people will find you soon enough," Lotus said. "Or that you've got some means of letting them know where you are. Also, I'll leave the vehicle where you can find it. I'm not a thief, you know."

Rather than speak, Fokine made a rude gesture in response, causing Lotus to laugh.

"Just remember what we talked about," Lotus said with a chuckle. With that, he prepared to get into the vehicle but was suddenly distracted by a bright flash of light.

The illumination seemed to come from an empty space in the middle of the garage, where it looked as though the air itself had been roughly hacked open. Lotus immediately recognized the phenomena as a dimensional rift; something was coming through. Or, more likely, some*one*.

Unsure of whether it was friend or foe, Lotus became quite keenly aware that the only weapon on his person was Fokine's gun. He frowned in disapproval; based on past experience, the weapon was unlikely to be useful if something threatening was about to make an appearance.

A moment later, a humanoid form stepped from the rift, colossal in both height and girth. Recognizing who it was, Lotus' shoulders slumped slightly as he relaxed and let out a sigh of relief.

"Really?" Lotus said to the new arrival. "*Now* you show up?"

Chapter 6

"What the hell is that?" Duncan said.

"That's Cerulean," Lotus replied. "He's an Eonian Enforcer."

"A what?" asked Desiree.

Lotus sighed. "It's a long story."

The three of them were currently in the great room of the Dreamborn home. Everyone had been out when Lotus had returned, accompanied by Cerulean, who now stood silent and unmoving in a corner of the room.

In short, the Enforcer had finally performed the act that Lotus had wanted done back on the black ops planet: he had opened a dimensional rift, which he had then used to travel to Fokine's garage. (How Cerulean actually knew where to go was something Lotus didn't have an answer to, although — since they were purportedly connected in some way — the Enforcer may have instinctively known where Lotus could be found.) Now that Duncan and the others were returning home, Lotus found himself trying to explain the presence of Cerulean without going into too much detail about how the colossus had come to be in his employ, for lack of a better term.

"Anyway," Lotus said, "he'll be coming with me, so you don't have to worry about him. And speaking of my departure…"

Lotus looked at his stepson expectantly.

"Yes, yes, I got the money," Duncan said. "Or rather, I gave the bank the instructions you provided. They're pretty complicated, so it's going to take the bank a little while to set everything up. That said, by this time tomorrow, through a series of complex and convoluted transactions and transfers, the funds will be waiting for you under the name Herlandous Ankh, just like you asked. And if the bank does everything right, the initial source of those funds — *me* — will be untraceable."

"Great," Lotus said. "And you've got the details of the account I left for you?"

"Yes."

"And you remember the story?"

"Yes, Dad," Duncan replied in an almost-exasperated voice. "If anyone asks, the funds in that account are to cover the purchase of an option you're making on our mineral rights. Other than that, none of us have ever seen you before."

Lotus nodded in satisfaction. "All right. Sounds good."

"You know," Desiree chimed in, "Collin's still not wild about our participation in this."

"Well, you can tell him I upheld my end of the bargain," Lotus declared. "You shouldn't have any more problems from the Zinnom Syndicate." Before he and Cerulean had left the sub-basement garage, Lotus had offered Fokine one last demonstration of what he could expect if they bumped heads again: he'd gotten the Enforcer to crush one of Fokine's vehicles, barehanded.

"But if you're worried about them, hire some additional security," Lotus continued. "You'll be able to afford it."

"Not until we make some kind of deal for our mineral rights," Desiree clarified. "And we're still fielding offers."

"Yeah, right," Lotus agreed. "Not until then. Right. Until you have a deal."

Duncan gave him an odd look, and Lotus realized it was because he had been rambling somewhat.

"Another option," Lotus said, trying to focus attention on something else, "you could always mine the kyzellium yourselves."

"Ha!" Duncan barked, chuckling. "We don't have the funds to make that sort of investment. The best we can hope for is to sell the mineral rights and collect royalties. Some company will get most of the profit, but we'll still have enough to make us one of the wealthiest families around."

"Well, maybe you can get the funds from an investor or something."

Duncan shrugged. "Maybe, but I wouldn't hold my breath."

Lotus was on the verge of making a comment when Collin came into the room, looking somewhat agitated and excited at the same time.

Collin greeted everyone casually (including Lotus, who usually only got a grunt from him), and then turned to his father. "Dad, I need to speak with you. In private."

"Okay," Duncan said, looking befuddled. A moment later, he and Collin left the room.

"What's that about?" Lotus asked.

"Your guess is as good as mine," Desiree said. "But as I said a few moments ago, Collin hasn't quite embraced the deal his father made with you."

"I know. He thinks it's an elaborate con."

"Is it?" she asked him bluntly. "I mean, I believe that you are who you say you are, but that doesn't mean you're not misleading Duncan."

He was about to respond when an odd two-tone musical note sounded, reverberating throughout the house. It took Lotus a moment to recognize it as the doorbell, unchanged since he'd first married Duncan's mother. While Desiree went to the front door to investigate, Lotus found himself reminiscing as long-dormant memories rose to the surface of his mind: guests arriving for dinner parties, children coming over for birthday celebrations, neighbors coming by just to say hello…

His reverie was interrupted when Desiree returned, carry a small box.

"There was no one there — just this," she said, indicating the box. "It's addressed to you."

"Me?" Lotus said, unable to keep the surprise out of his voice. "Nobody knows I'm here."

"Somebody does," Desiree countered, handing him the box.

Frowning, Lotus took the package from her. He looked for a label but didn't see one — just "Ian Lotus" handwritten on top. That didn't bode well — especially since he really hadn't gone by the Lotus moniker since escaping from the black ops world. Somebody definitely knew he was here.

Looking at the box itself, Lotus noticed that it wasn't particularly big — maybe a foot in length, half that in width, and an inch or so in breadth. He had a sneaking suspicion as to what the box contained, which was confirmed a moment later when he ripped it open to reveal a metal, rectangular device. Half of the thing's surface was covered with knobs, dials, and buttons, while the other side contained a number of flashing diodes arranged in a circle.

"A holo-comm," Desiree said. "I'm not sure I've seen one quite like that before."

Rather than respond, Lotus said, "Go get Duncan. And when you come back, stay out of the projector's range."

She nodded and left the room. Hitting one of the buttons on the device, Lotus was rewarded with a miniature hologram of Nicodemus appearing in the flashing circle.

"You need to leave Oasis," Nicodemus said, dispensing with the usual pleasantries. "They're on to you."

"Who?" Lotus asked.

"The Council. They know all about you — your non-terrestrial father, Eonian space, your half-brother Nigel. They know all of it."

"How? The only people who knew about it were you, Gourd, and Monica." He left unspoken his belief that none of those named would share his secrets.

"You're forgetting someone," Nicodemus said. "Wreath."

Lotus frowned. Harlan Wreath had been a wealthy and powerful media mogul. Stricken with a fatal disease, Wreath had made a deal with Lotus' half-brother, Nigel: Lotus' death in exchange for a cure. He'd also been so eager to survive that he'd been willing to let humanity be conquered by an invading alien armada if doing so could save his life.

"How can it be Wreath?" Lotus asked. "We left him stranded in my father's continuum. Even if he found a way back, he's basically a traitor. He almost got humanity wiped off the map. He'd be crazy to ever show his face again."

"I think the word you're looking for is 'eccentric.' You forget that he's incredibly wealthy, and he also had something to trade: information about you."

"So what, he bribed his way into a pardon of some sort with info about me and by lining the right pockets?"

"That's pretty much the gist of it. Now the Council is more desperate than ever to get their hands on you."

Lotus nodded in understanding. "So, how long before they get here?"

"Hard to say. They don't have access to the same information and resources that I do, but they know enough that it's really just a matter of time. At a guess, I'd say they're no more than a day behind me in tracking you down."

"That begs the question: exactly how did you find me?"

Nicodemus chuckled. "Since the early days, before mankind even left Earth, there was a saying with respect to how to locate just about anyone: follow the money. Although in your case, it was really more like, follow the *old* money. All I had to do was watch for activity in accounts that hadn't been touched in, say, thirty years or more."

Lotus ground his teeth in frustration. He hadn't expected anyone to be this hot on his trail. Still, this new info at least confirmed that he hadn't been paranoid with respect to funds; his pursuers were keeping watch on old accounts.

"Thanks for the heads-up, Nick," he finally said.

Nicodemus nodded. "Watch your ass."

The hologram disappeared. A second later, a crackling noise sounded from inside the holo-comm, followed by a small wisp of smoke rising from the device — a clear indication that vital internal components had been destroyed.

Motion in his peripheral vision drew Lotus' attention, and he looked up to see Duncan, Desiree, and Collin standing near the entryway into the room. He didn't know how long they'd been standing there, but they had obviously adhered to his instructions to stay out of range of the holo-comm's projectors.

Duncan and his wife were both looking at Lotus with concern. Collin, however, had a sheepish expression on his face, one that could almost be interpreted as guilt over something. Seeing him, understanding suddenly dawned on Lotus, and with it came barely-contained ire. He stalked over to the trio.

"What did you do?" Lotus demanded, his question overtly directed at Collin.

"Listen, Dad," Duncan began. "He didn't real—"

"No, Duncan," Lotus said firmly, cutting his stepson off. "He's had no problem being vocal up to this point. Let him speak for himself."

Duncan looked as if he wanted to say more, but something about the look on Lotus' face made him stay silent. Instead, he turned to Collin and said, "Go ahead, son."

On his part, Collin looked embarrassed — more like a schoolboy caught passing a dirty note than a man almost forty years old. Finally, he took a deep breath and began speaking.

"I just…I just wanted to be sure, that's all," he began. "I wanted to be certain you weren't running a scam."

"Go on," Lotus said.

"So, I took the account info you gave us and went to a bank — just to make sure there was actually money in it."

"And?" Desiree asked.

"Mom, there's almost eight *billion* in that account!" Collin said excitedly.

Desiree went bug-eyed. It was a mind-boggling amount of money, a fortune on a scale she could scarcely have imagined — even accounting for the sale of their kyzellium rights. She glanced at her husband, who didn't seem surprised at all, before realizing that this was probably what Collin had wanted to talk to him about. She then turned to Lotus, who was still frowning in displeasure.

Of course, the amount of money mentioned hadn't come as a surprise to him; after all, he was leaving this account to her, Duncan, and the rest of their family. He'd known what was in it. There was something else obviously bothering him.

"What else?" Lotus asked Collin. "Based on what I just heard on the holo-comm, there's more to the story. There has to be."

Collin briefly lowered his eyes in shame, and then softly announced, "There is. I transferred some funds."

Lotus drew in a harsh breath before asking his next question. "How much?"

For a moment, Collin's mouth worked without benefit of sound. He glanced nervously at his parents, as if for support, and then calmly said, "One hundred million credits!"

"Collin!" his mother practically screamed, unable to suppress her shock. At the same time, Lotus groaned audibly in frustration, wiping his face with his hand. "Why would you do that?"

"Because we aren't supposed to access it until he leaves!" Collin replied. "Just because the money's there now doesn't mean it'll be waiting after he's gone."

"But a hundred million?" Desiree continued. "That's way more — exponentially more — than we're loaning to him!"

"I guess I just got carried away," Collin admitted, chagrinned. "But he did say that everything in the account was supposed to be ours."

Three sets of eyes turned in Lotus direction.

"So this is why you mentioned us hiring security," Duncan surmised. "And being able to fund our own mining operation. You were planning on leaving us a fortune."

"I don't care about the money," Lotus replied. "I've got plenty more where that came from. The problem — as you probably overheard from my holographic conversation — is that it can be used to track me if I'm not careful."

"And we just screwed that up," Duncan concluded.

"*I* screwed it up, you mean," Collin said.

"It doesn't matter, but now we've got to rejigger our plans," Lotus said. "First off, immediately cancel the funds transfer. Now that people know where to look, they might be able to trace the money after all. Also, our story is changing. You've still never seen me before, but the money in the account is for an outright purchase of your minerals, not an option."

"Got it," Duncan said with a nod. "But what about you? Don't you still need money?"

"I've got other accounts I can probably access safely, now that I know the time frame my pursuers are looking at," Lotus replied. "I may have to make the banks jump through a few hoops to hide my tracks, but it can be done."

"I don't understand," Collin said. "If you actually have other accounts with as much money as you say, why go through the bother of getting a loan from us?"

"Don't you get it?" Duncan interjected. "None of this was really to get money *from* us. It was to give money *to* us. He's giving us the billions in that account."

Lotus sighed in resignation. "You never would have taken it if I'd just offered. But this way…"

"This way," Desiree said, after Lotus trailed off, "once you were gone and we found out what was in the account, there'd be no way to refuse."

"But why?" Duncan asked Lotus. "You and Mom left me way more than enough, as well as trust funds and an investment portfolio."

Lotus shrugged. "I guess I still feel guilty about the way I left. I thought it'd make up for me just deserting you like that."

"Dad, you didn't desert me," Duncan assured him. "You went after Mom. It's the same thing I'd do today if something similar happened to Desiree."

Lotus smiled in relief. "Thanks, son."

"So what now?" Collin asked.

"Now I leave," Lotus answered. "The sooner the better, in fact."

As if to punctuate his statement, a bright flash suddenly appeared in the middle of the room — two of them, in fact. Dimensional rifts.

"What is that?" Duncan asked, shading his eyes with his hand.

"Get out," Lotus said in response, rather than directly answering the question. "All of you. Leave. Right now."

At the same time, Cerulean took a step forward from his stance in the corner, seemingly on edge.

An enormous humanoid form began stepping through the first rift, and then the second. Even before they were fully through, Lotus recognized them for what they were: Eonian Enforcers.

Noting that Duncan, Collin, and Desiree were still standing there, he screamed, "Go!"

His shout seemed to break their fascination with the rifts, as well as (more importantly) convey the sentiment that they were in danger. At Lotus' urging, the other three fled the room.

In all honesty, Lotus should have been right on their heels. He'd bumped heads with an Enforcer before and was under no illusions that he was any kind of match for one of them. That said, he'd never seen two of them coming through rifts before. (Frankly speaking, it seemed like overkill, since *one* Enforcer was practically unstoppable.)

A moment later, the light from the rifts faded, leaving only the two new arrivals, both of whom turned towards Lotus. Neither of them was Obsidian — the Enforcer Lotus had faced several times previously and who served his half-brother Nigel. Thus, it momentarily crossed Lotus' mind that maybe these were friendlies. All such thoughts vanished a moment later, however, when one of the Enforcers took a menacing step towards him and — finding its path blocked by a sofa — flung the couch aside with such force that it went halfway through the wall.

{*Alive!*} said an odd, disembodied voice that Lotus seemed to only hear inside his head. {*I need him alive.*}

Lotus shook his head slightly to clear it. This wasn't the first time he'd heard mental orders being given to an Enforcer, although his ability to do so was purportedly very rare. In addition, the person giving the orders wouldn't know that Lotus was listening in, so to speak.

The two new Enforcers had frozen while the ethereal voice (which sounded feminine) had spoken. Now they went back into motion, heading towards Lotus. However, they had apparently forgotten about (or, more appropriately, probably never noticed) Cerulean, who came behind them. Cerulean then grabbed one of the new arrivals, lifted him, and then slammed him back down onto the floor hard enough to send tremors through the house. Lotus watched as his companion then grabbed the downed Enforcer by the leg, spun, and then flung him through one of the exterior walls.

The other new arrival swung a meaty fist at Cerulean's face, connecting with enough force to fell an elephant. Cerulean staggered back a step, and then came forward swinging a haymaker of his own. A moment later, the two behemoths were going at each other, with blows ringing out like hammers on steel.

Over the din of fisticuffs, Lotus' ears picked up the sound of wood splintering. Turning in the direction of the noise, he saw the Enforcer that Cerulean had flung through the wall trying to enter the house through the hole his body had made. Lotus had been so engrossed watching Cerulean's current battle that he had almost forgotten about this other combatant.

Looking for something to use as a weapon, Lotus spied a full complement of tools meant for a fireplace that currently sat in the family room: a metal poker, shovel, broom, and more. Grabbing the poker, he charged at the Enforcer who was making his way back into the house, seemingly intent on smashing the thing's face in. At the last second, however, he feinted, coming in low instead to avoid a grab by the Enforcer and bashing his opponent on the knee.

The effect on the Enforcer was negligible; it didn't even seem to grunt in response to the blow. The poker, however, folded like tinfoil. Lotus tossed the useless piece of metal aside in disgust, and then began backing up warily as the Enforcer he'd just engaged began to close on him.

Before it could take more than a few steps, however, something crashed into it with the force of a locomotive, sending the Enforcer tumbling back out through the hole in the wall. Glancing out the opening, Lotus saw what had hit his opponent: the other Enforcer that Cerulean had been fighting. Apparently, Cerulean had managed to fling his own assailant into its companion.

It was a tactic that had bought them a few seconds, at most; their two attackers were already getting back on their feet. Moreover, the longer they fought here, the more likely it was that Duncan or someone in his family was likely to get hurt. They needed to move the field of play somehow.

Lotus barely had time to process this before he found himself lifted bodily from the floor. Instantly anxious, he only relaxed slightly when he saw that it was Cerulean who held him. Cradling Lotus like a baby, the colossus turned and charged towards one of the other, intact walls of the house.

"No!" Lotus screamed, then closed his eyes and braced for the shock of impact.

Chapter 7

The expected impact never came. Instead, through his closed lids, Lotus sensed a brilliant flash of light. The next thing he knew, his ears were being assaulted by an unexpected cacophony of sound. He heard the chirps of birds, mingled with the buzz of insects and the chatter of various animals.

Timidly, Lotus opened his eyes as Cerulean set him down. He was in a small clearing in some kind of tropical environment, albeit one covered in violet rather than green plants. Oppressive heat and humidity began bearing down on him immediately, and — as he noted that the leaves of a nearby plant bore an unnerving resemblance to human hands — he realized that he had been here before (although his last visit had been decades earlier).

The planet was known as Menagerie IX. As the name implied (and due to the abundance of unique life forms found there), it was really more of a nature preserve, with only a few human habitations. As his ears had confirmed earlier, there were all kinds of animals surrounding them.

Lotus didn't waste much thought on figuring out how they'd gotten here. Apparently, rather than continuing to fight the two Enforcers, Cerulean had opened a rift and transported them. Discretion being the better part of valor, Lotus had no issue with his companion's actions. However, they seriously needed to consider their next move, because—

Lotus' thoughts were interrupted by twin flares of light appearing not far away from them. A moment later, the two Enforcers they had just fought were standing about ten yards away. (At least, Lotus assumed it was the same two, as they were dressed the same — one in green, the other in blue — as the two that had attacked them at the Dreamborn family home. Truth be told, he hadn't spent much time studying their facial features.)

Cerulean launched himself at the other two Enforcers. Soon, blows were echoing through the jungle around them as the titans fought, with the battle being made all the more eerie by the fact that the combatants barely made a sound.

Lotus wanted to join the fray, to help in some manner, but realized that he'd do little more than get in the way. Despite his bulk, Cerulean seemed to be a talented fighter, managing to keep his two attackers off-balance with well-timed feints and punches. That said, he was clearly on the defensive, as he had to continually move strategically in order to keep his opponents in sight and avoid being outflanked.

A harsh animal cry penetrated the air, and Lotus — recognizing the scream of a predator — spun in the direction of the noise. He saw nothing before him but thick, lush vegetation. However, he noticed a quivering in the foliage, a shaking in the underbrush that seemed to move from one plant to another in a direct line towards him, like a powerful wind blowing through them in his direction.

Lotus instinctively knew that there was some kind of animal in the underbrush, and that it was charging straight at him. By all indications it was large, and quite likely in attack mode. A moment later, it broke into the clearing.

As Lotus had suspected, the animal was big — about waist-high and around three hundred pounds. Six-legged and looking like a cross between a razorback and a shark, it came barreling towards Lotus, growling fiercely.

Frantically, Lotus dove aside to avoid the animal's charge. He hit the ground, rolled, and came up into a sitting position — only to find the beast bearing down on him again. He began hastily scuttling backwards as the animal advanced, snapping at his legs and feet.

Worried that he might be getting too close to Cerulean's fight with the two attackers, Lotus suddenly changed tactics. Taking care to time it just right, he extended a leg and then swung it in a powerful kick at the animal's chin. It yelped and then dropped to the ground on its side, stunned and with its mouth lolling open.

Wasting no time, Lotus scrambled on top of the beast. Taking a calculated risk, he reached into the animal's mouth with his hands and — getting a grip on its upper and lower jaw — began pulling them as hard as possible in opposite directions.

The pain of having its mouth forcefully pried open seemed to bring the animal around. Grunting in anguish, it tried to rise, but Lotus' weight kept it pinned down. It bucked and flailed its limbs, striking Lotus in the ribs at one point, but he refused to release his grip. The creature began mewling in distress as muscle and sinew seemed to give under Lotus' assault. A moment later, there was a harsh cracking sound and the animal's cries stopped. At the same time, Lotus felt the thing's upper jaw suddenly go slack in his grip. Breathing heavily, he rolled off the animal, which began to spasm wildly as it went into its death throes.

He had only lain there a second before he heard another primordial scream, this one even more sonorous than that of the animal he'd just killed. A moment later, the ground quivering under its feet, a monstrosity lumbered into the clearing.

It was taller at the shoulder than Lotus and massive in size. Overall, however, its general appearance was like that of the slain beast next to him, sort of a shark-boar. Noting that, the facts of the situation quickly aligned themselves in such a way that Lotus had no trouble understanding the predicament he now found himself in. The animal he had just killed had been a cub, a baby. Now he had to deal with Momma…

Apparently seeing its offspring lying unmoving next to Lotus, the larger animal let out another deafening roar and charged at him. Lotus scrambled to his feet and made a mad dash towards the area where Cerulean was still taking on the other two Enforcers. He knew there was no way he could take on the parent barehanded, as he'd done the cub; his best hope was to somehow distract the raging beast, and putting a trio of titans engaged in fisticuffs between him and it seemed like the best solution at the moment.

Cerulean was still holding his own against his two adversaries. Lotus, attempting to skirt the outer edge of what he interpreted as being their area of engagement, spared a glance back to see how close he was to being trampled and eaten. It was a nigh-fatal error. While there seemed to be adequate distance between him and the charging animal, looking behind left him open to being blindsided — which is exactly what happened when one of the attacking Enforcers drew back his arm to throw a punch at Cerulean. A hefty elbow slammed into the side of Lotus' head, sending him tumbling into the underbrush.

Lotus lay on the ground, slightly dazed. Not far away, he heard the large animal bellow again, a sound of maddened grief and anguish. The ground, however, was no longer shaking, which meant the creature was no longer running. Had it found him? Was he seconds away from being stomped into the ground?

Shaking his head to clear his thoughts, Lotus slowly sat up, realizing as he did so that he was surrounded on all sides by purple foliage. That fact alone made it unlikely that he had been found by the beast that had been chasing him. Peeking out, he saw — to his surprise — two battles raging at once.

On the one hand, Cerulean was in a one-on-one battle with the Enforcer that was dressed in green. (And now that it was more of a fair fight, Lotus was happy to see that his companion seemed to be the more skilled combatant.) At the same time, the other Enforcer, in blue, was battling the shark-boar animal; the beast had bitten down on its opponent's right arm and seemed intent on trying to gnaw the limb off, while the Enforcer hammered at it with his free hand. In truth, Lotus was hard-pressed to guess as to who would win the fight, although from personal experience he gave the edge to the Enforcer.

Getting to his feet, Lotus once again decided, after assessing the scene before him, that intervening in any fashion was only likely to get him killed. Besides, the only one of the four combatants he'd be willing to help was Cerulean, who seemed to be more than holding his own. He just wished his gargantuan companion would hurry and wrap things up. They needed to get out of here, although he didn't have a firm idea in mind of where they should go.

Suddenly, Cerulean landed a wicked combination of punches, momentarily stunning his opponent. He then grabbed his adversary, lifted him up, and then slammed him into the ground hard enough to cause tremors. Cerulean then spun and dashed towards Lotus, coming at him so fast that Lotus thought he'd be crushed. His immediate thought was to wave both hands above his head to make sure that his companion saw him. Before he could do so, however, Cerulean was there; almost without breaking stride, he picked Lotus up, tossed him over his shoulder in a fireman's carry, and kept running. A moment later, light flashed around them, and Lotus realized they had stepped into another dimensional rift.

Chapter 8

They came out into what felt like a blast furnace. They were in the middle of a desert of some sort, with nothing but sand and dunes in all directions, as far as the eye could see. Lotus had thought the heat on Menagerie was oppressive, but — within moments, as sweat began to pour off him — he realized that it was a summer breeze compared to their present environs. Shielding his eyes, he looked up at the sky and saw the culprit: a binary star.

The sight of the twin suns made Lotus keenly aware of a new fact. As with Menagerie, he realized that he had been to this planet before. It was an inhospitable desert world known as Arid Hope, and to be frank, Lotus was less than thrilled to be here. He couldn't speak for Cerulean, but without supplies (especially water), the heat of this planet would cook a man in hours. That being the case, locating a water source was his number-one priority.

Or maybe number two, Lotus thought, as he noticed light spilling out of a couple of fissures that had just opened in the air before them. He didn't need a guess as to who was joining them, and was thus not surprised to see the two Enforcers they'd just left behind. They looked a little banged up, sporting what appeared to be bruises here and there, but were far from being down for the count.

As before, Cerulean placed himself between Lotus and the newly-arrived Enforcers. As Lotus watched, the three of them resumed the same song-and-dance number they'd been doing before the beast on Menagerie had apparently burst into their midst.

From Lotus' perspective, this pattern that was developing — he and Cerulean fleeing from one world to the next, with these two pursuing them — was going to get old fast. It wasn't clear yet how the two Enforcers were following them, but it obviously related to Eonian science or technology in some way. What they needed was some place they could get to where their foes wouldn't or couldn't follow. If they could just—

{*Now!*} said an ethereal voice — the same one that Lotus had heard before back on Oasis. {*Get him!*}

Something like an oversized vise closed on Lotus, pinning his arms to his sides as he was lifted from the ground. Looking over his shoulder, he saw what — unfortunately — he was expecting: a third Enforcer, this one dressed in yellow.

Lotus wanted to kick himself. He had fallen for one of the oldest ruses in the book. He'd allowed the battle between Cerulean and their initial attackers to distract him. Being less than vigilant, he had seemingly failed to notice that a third dimensional rift had opened behind him at some point. More to the point, this particular rift was still open, and Lotus' captor started walking back towards it with Lotus in tow.

"Put me down, asshole!" Lotus shouted, kicking his legs maniacally (since they were the only body parts he could move). To his great surprise, the Enforcer carrying him paused, and then — after spending a few moments standing completely still, like a statue — actually complied with the request.

As for Lotus, he stood frozen for a moment himself. To say he was surprised that there had been compliance with his demand would have been an understatement. He was, in truth, stunned. He certainly hadn't expected his captor to release him; it had just been the usual rhetoric one typically shouted in those situations. Like a criminal in handcuffs screaming for an arresting officer to let him go, he hadn't actually expected it to happen. Now that it had, he was having trouble processing exactly what it meant.

His time to dwell on the subject came to an abrupt end, however, as Cerulean — racing over — slammed a shoulder into Lotus' captor that sent him bouncing across the dunes. Cerulean then grabbed Lotus, who expected to be carried through yet another rift across the shoulder of his companion. Much to his shock and surprise, instead of carrying him, Cerulean flung him away like a rag doll.

Chapter 9

Lotus had been so caught off guard by Cerulean's actions that he didn't even have time to protest. Flying through the air, an image flashed across his mind of himself skidding across the desert's burning sands, thereby picking up a serious case of road rash.

That scenario, however, never materialized. Instead, the scene changed jarringly, going from the desert at midday to a bleak, gray landscape framed by a bulbous orange sun that was either setting or rising on the horizon. His brain immediately processed the fact that Cerulean had apparently tossed him through another dimensional rift.

It was noticeably cooler here, which meant that he probably wouldn't end up being turned into a piece of human jerky. That said, he had a more immediate problem: he seemed to have come through the rift in midair, and was now falling.

Fortunately, he didn't have time to panic, as a second later he landed in some body of water — probably a lake or a river. He must have fallen from a fairly distant height, because hitting the surface was like being slammed into the side of a tank, with the impact driving all the air from his lungs. Somewhat disoriented and fighting the pain, he sank for a moment before getting his arms and legs moving.

Seconds later, he broke the surface, sputtering and wheezing for breath. He felt himself being pushed along, thereby concluding that he had probably landed in a river. Moreover, while his eyes hadn't fully adjusted to the dim light, the roar of rushing water ahead told him that he was about to hit some rapids. Glancing around, he picked the riverbank side that — based on the outline of the trees against the sky — looked closest, and began swimming perpendicular to the flow of the river as fast as he could in that direction.

Ten minutes later (and farther downstream), he dragged himself — battered and bruised from the rapids — out of the water and collapsed, exhausted, on the bank.

He lay there, eyes closed, intending to rest only for a moment before assessing his surroundings. Within moments, he was asleep.

****

Lotus woke to an unfamiliar sensation, but not one that was foreign to his experience: being roughly dragged across the ground by his heels. His vision was a little hazy, but he could make out someone in a hooded cloak shambling backwards as they gripped him by the ankles.

Taking advantage of the element of surprise, Lotus drew his right knee in suddenly, yanking his foot free, and then shot the leg forward in a kick that landed on his erstwhile abductor's chest. The person grunted in pain at the unexpected blow, which caused them to release their grip and flop backwards onto the ground.

Lotus drew in his legs and rolled back onto his shoulders. Placing his hands on the ground by his head, he then performed a kip-up, flipping up onto his feet in a kneeling position. He then dove towards the person he had kicked, landing on top of them and pinning them to the ground. Lotus drew back his fist in anticipation of throwing a punch, and then realized something. The person he was about to slug was a girl.

She was perhaps fifteen years old, with a comely face surrounded by dark, curly hair. Her eyes, wide as saucers in light of Lotus' aggression, seemed to be green with flecks of gold in them. In a clear move of submission, her hands lay flat and open on the ground next to her, showing that she had no weapon.

As Lotus recovered from his surprise, the fingers of his fisted hand slowly loosened. Seeing this, the girl said something, speaking softly but audibly; the language, however, was foreign to him. She grunted and bucked slightly, and Lotus realized she was telling him to get off her. Muttering an apology (which she probably didn't understand), he did so.

The girl sat up and then slowly rose to her feet, as did Lotus. She looked at him and then said something, circling a finger in his direction as if to indicate him in his entirety. While he still didn't understand what she was saying, her words seemed to initiate some kind of buzzing in his brains. It was as if a hive of bees was in his head, and something had happened to make them agitated.

Wincing more in annoyance than in pain, he began massaging his temples with his fingertips. As the girl continued to speak, the buzzing grew louder, drowning out all other sound. Lotus spared the girl a glance; she was still speaking and looking at him with concern on her face, but he couldn't even hear her voice over the droning between his ears.

And then, just as quickly as it had arrived, the buzzing began to fade. However, as the noise died down and his hearing returned, another fact became evident. He could now understand the girl.

"—sing," she said.

"I'm sorry," Lotus said. "I didn't catch that."

"I said the river is rising," she repeated. "You didn't seem to want to wake up, so I was trying to get you to higher ground."

She pointed behind him, and Lotus turned to look. It now seemed to be daytime, and he could see a trail in the dirt (indicating where he had been dragged) leading from the riverside to their present location atop an embankment near a heavily-wooded forest. As he watched, he saw the river swelling and realized that the girl had been telling the truth. There had perhaps been a storm or some other event farther upstream that was causing the river to expand beyond its normal boundaries. Presumably the rising water would have roused him from his sleep, but there was also a chance that he would have gotten washed away if a big enough surge came along. In short, the girl might have saved his life.

He looked at the girl. "Thank you. I'm Ian Lotus, by the way."

She acknowledged his gratitude with a nod, and then hooked a thumb at herself. "Matreen bao-Negoy." Then, looking him over critically, she asked, "Where do you come from?"

Lotus chuckled. "The answer to that is a little tricky. I'm not sure how best to respond."

She did the twirling motion with her fingers again. "Your garb is unusual. I don't think I've seen anything quite like it before."

Looking down, Lotus noticed that he was still wearing the one-piece from his meeting with Fokine. It seemed as though that interlude had taken place ages ago, but in truth it had been, what — maybe a day? And where was he that a simple one-piece was unusual?

Before he could ask, Matreen grabbed his arm and ducked down in a crouching position behind a nearby bush, pulling him down with her. As Lotus started to protest, she made a shushing sound and then pointed to the river.

Looking where indicated, Lotus didn't initially see anything. A moment later, however, a small airboat — floating a few feet above the water — came zipping down the center of the river from somewhere upstream. From what Lotus could see, the vehicle, which could perhaps hold a maximum of six people, was occupied by two armored (and armed) men and an Enforcer.

Lotus couldn't tell if this was some kind of scouting mission or merely a patrol. Regardless, he and Matreen stayed out of sight until the craft disappeared around a bend in the river.

"Come," Matreen said, and then began walking towards the forest.

Mind brimming with questions, Lotus followed her.

Chapter 10

As he trailed Matreen through the forest, Lotus tried to get more information about his whereabouts. Unlike the two prior planets Cerulean's rift had taken him to, nothing about his current location jogged any portion of Lotus' memory — not the birds, not the greenery, not the landscape. Moreover, Matreen's responses to his questions on the subject were maddening.

"This is the Infinituum," she would casually respond, as if that answered everything. In fact, it was the same answer he'd get, no matter how he phrased the question.

"What world is this?"

"This is the Infinituum."

"Does this planet have a name?"

"This is the Infinituum."

"Is this world known by any other moniker?"

"This is the Infinituum."

On the flip side, she seemed just as befuddled by his answers to questions about where he was from. Plainly speaking, she seemed incapable of conceiving of any world outside the "Infinituum," as she put it.

"All these locations you cite," she'd said, speaking of several planets Lotus had mentioned visiting. "They are all unfamiliar to me as tracts within the Infinituum."

After a while, Lotus had decided they'd make more progress talking about other subjects.

"Where are we going?" he asked.

"My village," she replied. "We'll be safe there."

"Safe from what?"

She gave him an odd look. "The Sentinels, of course. They probably would have taken you had they come across you dozing, as I did."

Her words brought to mind the guards and Enforcer he had seen on the airboat.

"They would have taken me?" he asked quizzically. "Taken me where?"

Matreen looked at him as though he were a tree that had learned to speak. "They would have taken you back to serve the Great Infinity, of course. Surely you know this."

Lotus shook his head. "How about this? Instead of looking at me like I'm a moronic dickhead every time I ask you a question, why don't we just pretend I just awoke from a thousand-year sleep and am trying to get my bearings."

"It would not matter. A thousand years, two thousand, ten thousand. The Great Infinity has ruled since time immemorial, with no change to the Canon of Laws."

"Wait a minute," Lotus said, frowning. "This 'Infinity' you keep mentioning — it's a person?"

"Not as you or I would define it. Infinity is power personified."

Lotus frowned in thought. This Infinity sounded a lot like his father. Was Infinity simply another name for Eon? Was he actually in his father's continuum? Admittedly, he didn't see much other than the palace when he was there before, but he hadn't gotten the sense of his father's realm being anything like his current environs.

"You mentioned that the Sentinels might have taken me to serve Infinity," Lotus said. "Did you mean like a slave?"

Matreen shrugged. "It's not clear. Those taken are seldom reported as being seen again, although legend has it that — far in the past — a few did indeed return."

"So Sentinels have the authority to just snatch up anyone they like and take them away?"

Matreen shook her head. "Normally they confine their selections to the oblations offered by the towns and villages."

"Oblations?" Lotus repeated. "You mean you willingly offer up your own people to be slaves?"

"Infinity provides all that we need — sunshine, rain, bountiful land. Exchanging a few of our fellows for that is very much a bargain."

Lotus couldn't help but note that she spoke those last sentences in an emotionless voice, as if she didn't really believe them. It was more as if she was quoting something that she had learned by rote rather than expressing how she truly felt.

"Besides," she continued, "Infinity also protects us from the Dark Foe."

"The what?"

"The Dark Foe — the ancient enemy of our people."

"And that's his name — the Dark Foe?"

"He has a name, but it is forbidden to speak it. Infinity has spent ages amassing an army to challenge him for supremacy."

Lotus went silent, contemplating what he had heard. He could very well see his father being worshipped and ruling under another name. However, little else that

Matreen had shared comported with his own perception of Eon and the realm he held sway over. As he continued following Matreen through the forest, he decided that he definitely needed more information, although it wasn't clear where he could get it.

Chapter 11

It took about two hours for them to reach Matreen's village, which seemingly was home to several hundred people. To be precise, it was Matreen's house that they initially arrived at, which was a few miles from the village square.

Matreen, it turned out, was the oldest of five siblings who still lived at home with their parents. (Two older sisters had married and moved away a few years earlier.) The house itself was a two-story structure that turned out to be a fair size larger than Lotus had anticipated.

Matreen's mother and father, Leva and Norel, were more than surprised to see their daughter return with a guest, although they quickly made Lotus feel welcome. They found some clean clothes for him to wear, and then Norel showed him to a bathroom and shower on the second floor that he could use.

A short time later, Lotus emerged showered and refreshed, as well as wearing clean clothes. The house, however, seemed rather quiet, and he didn't see anyone around.

"Hello?" Lotus said softly as he stepped towards the stairs with the dirty one-piece in his hand. He wasn't quite sure what to do with it, but didn't want to just leave it lying around like he expected the maid to pick it up. Not getting an answer to his tentative greeting, he went down to the first floor.

The room at the bottom of the stairs seemed to be a den. Once there, Lotus didn't immediately see anyone, but he thought he could hear voices down a hallway to the left of the stairs. With no other options, he headed down the corridor.

The hallway led him past a couple of closed doors and terminated in what appeared to be a kitchen. As he entered, he saw a highly animated Norel speaking in hushed tones with another man.

The other man was younger than Norel, and gave the appearance of being in his mid-thirties. He was roughly Lotus' height but bulkier, like he spent a lot of time lifting weights. Neither man immediately noticed Lotus, who watched them having what was apparently a very serious debate for a moment before announcing his presence by clearing his throat. Their conversation came to an abrupt halt as both men looked in his direction.

"I apologize for intruding," Lotus said, "but I didn't see anyone else around. If you could tell me where I could wash this" — he held up his one-piece — "I'll ju—"

"Nonsense," Norel said, cutting him off. "Just toss it in the corner there."

"Thanks," Lotus said, placing the one-piece where indicated.

"Now, let me introduce you to one of the village councilors," Norel said, indicating the man he had been speaking to. "This is Thoban. Thoban, this is Lotus."

Lotus extended a hand. "Pleased to meet you."

Frowning, Thoban looked at Lotus' hand, then at Norel, then at Lotus' face, and finally his hand again. Feeling foolish, Lotus withdrew his hand, at which point Thoban made a gesture that Lotus recognized as a greeting among his father's people.

So there is a connection to Eon, he thought as he returned the gesture.

"Unfortunately, Thoban was just leaving, as he only stopped by to remind me of a village meeting later."

"Yes," said Thoban as he stepped towards a door that led from the kitchen to the outside. "I hope we'll see you there, Norel."

Norel nodded as he showed Thoban out, promising that he would be at the meeting.

"I'm sorry," Lotus began after Thoban was gone. "I didn't mean to wander through your home, but I didn't see anyone."

"It's fine," Norel assured him. "My wife and the children had to go out."

"Oh. Well, thank you again for the use of the shower."

Norel chuckled. "You sound surprised that we have such a luxury."

Lotus smiled. "Frankly, I am. From Matreen, I somehow gathered that villages like yours were in an agrarian, pre-industrial state."

"Not exactly. We tend to live simple lives, but are not completely without modern conveniences or knowledge of technology."

"Then I apologize for my poor assumptions."

"No need. You're obviously a stranger here, as evident from your garments."

"Yes. And thanks also for the clothes," Lotus added, indicating the long-sleeved tunic and pants he was wearing. "Although, I must admit to being surprised that you had my size." This last statement alluded to the fact that Lotus was at least a head taller than Norel.

The older man was silent for a moment, then sighed despondently. "They're my son's clothes."

"Oh. Is he around?"

"No, he..." A faraway look came into Norel's eyes. "He... The Sentinels took him."

Lotus remained quiet, not sure of what to say, and then offered his condolences.

"It's fine," Norel assured him. "It's been awhile since it happened, but still, some days are better than others in terms of coping. Besides, it's no more than what we've had to endure as a people for ages."

"Do you know what they do with them?"

"All we have are rumors and speculation. The most popular theory is that they are conscripts, forced to join the legions who will one day fight in Infinity's coming battle with the Dark Foe."

Lotus nodded. "Forced induction into the military is not completely unknown among my people either, although typically such draftees are still allowed to communicate with friends and family."

Norel gave him an appraising stare. "So, you really are from outside the Infinituum."

"I take it that's unusual. Matreen spoke as if the Infinituum was all that there was."

Norel laughed. "I'm sure she was simply being circumspect. It is part of the canon that is enforced, so — not knowing who you were — she simply recited the dogma we are all required to learn."

"So what's changed so that you're telling me this now?"

"There's a legend, a prophecy, which says that when the time of the Great Battle draws near, one would come from beyond the Infinituum to stop our persecution."

Lotus laughed. Like most prophecies, it was somewhat ambiguous, and he said as much. "Trust me, every battle is the 'great one' when you're in it. Regardless, does that mean a battle with this Dark Foe you mentioned or someone else? Is it talking about persecution at the hands of this unnamed enemy or Infinity? In all honesty, it's a little difficult to get your arms around."

"What you say is true, but I've seen much in my life that gives me reason to believe the prophecy will, in time, be fulfilled. Others, however, grow weary of waiting."

Lotus' brow furrowed as he contemplated what Norel had inferred. "Wait a minute. What are you saying?"

Norel merely stared at him, and Lotus could almost see the wheels turning in the man's mind as he contemplated his next action and words. Clearly, he was making some weighty decision, and it seemed to involve Lotus. Finally, he seemed to come to some conclusion.

"Come with me," Norel said.

Chapter 12

"Should you be showing me this?" Lotus asked.

"Maybe, maybe not," Norel said. "But if you *are* the prophecy come to life, then it's important that you know that others have the will and the means to support your campaign."

"Let's be clear about something," Lotus said. "There is no campaign."

Norel shrugged. "So you say now."

They were in Norel's barn, an expansive structure that was used to store various types of equipment and grain, as well as house several farm animals that Lotus, in his own mind, would have classified as exotic. Norel had led him to an empty stall at the rear of the building where, after activating some controller that Lotus never saw, the floor had opened up and a rectangular platform had arisen. On it was what appeared to be a robot, and — judging from its armor and weaponry — it was clearly designed for battle.

"So this is a rebellion," Lotus surmised, after finishing his inspection of the robot.

"Not at the moment," Norel corrected. "We've yet to take any real action, only assembled weapons and constructed automatons, like this."

Seeing the 'bot on the table, which Norel claimed to have built, Lotus was once again forced to revise his assessment of how technologically advanced these people were.

"This is impressive," Lotus finally stated aloud.

"Thank you," Norel said with a humble smile. "It's difficult to ascertain from our lifestyle, but we have the knowledge base and technical expertise to do these things and much, much more. What we lack is resources."

"What do you mean?"

"Metals, minerals, and such — almost anything with utility other than food — is requisitioned in its totality by Infinity. Ostensibly, it is so that we can continue preparing for the battle against the Dark Foe by building weapons and war machines."

"But the practical effect is that it keeps people like you and your village pretty much defenseless and incapable of making trouble."

"Your insights are more correct that you realize. It is forbidden for anyone to construct an automaton like this. Infinity's forces would raze our village to the ground if they knew and make examples of us all."

"Which goes back to my original question: should you be showing me this?"

Norel seemed to reflect on the question for a second, then said, "We've waited a long time for this prophesied liberator, and — although there have been stories of those arriving from outside the Infinituum — you are the first time I believe it can be confirmed."

"So in other words, it's now or never with respect to this prophecy."

"More or less."

"Aren't you worried about failing? About this village being wiped off the map if your actions are discovered?"

"The Sentinels are taking oblations — our children — more and more frequently now. Soon there won't be a village left regardless of what we do."

"I see."

Once again without Lotus noticing, Norel must have triggered a controller of some sort, because the platform began to lower again. A moment later, the floor slid back into place.

"Now, I must leave for this meeting," Norel stated. "My wife is meeting me there, but Matreen and the other children will return soon."

"Would it be too much of a stretch to assume this meeting is about me?"

Norel smiled. "Not a stretch at all."

"I'm curious about something. I didn't spend much time in the shower, but Thoban was already here when I came out. That implies that he already knew about me and was on his way here before Matreen and I even arrived."

"We have sentries, in the forest and beyond. Word was passed along about your pending arrival almost as soon as you and my daughter began heading in our direction."

Lotus was almost tempted to ask how, but realized that there must be dozens of ways to communicate over long distances, whether you have advanced technology or not. Even on Old Earth, where he was originally from, people had used things such as mirrors and smoke signals to send messages almost instantly from miles away.

"So now you go to decide if I'm the legend come to life," Lotus said.

"More or less," Norel said. "Although most will probably have to see you for themselves before they can believe it."

"And how will they know I'm not just some guy simply claiming to be the person in the prophecy?"

Norel laughed. "Anyone seeing you won't make that mistake. I haven't mentioned it, but you have certain idiosyncrasies, including mannerisms and expressions, that — plainly speaking — are quite foreign."

Lotus nodded in understanding, remembering his attempt to shake Thoban's hand. More to the point, he had also noticed certain quirks in the behavior of his newfound friends, but had not found them worth noting to any great extent.

"So you're telling me I should look forward to getting poked and prodded in the near future."

Norel chuckled again. "Something like that."

Chapter 13

"Did you hear something?" Matreen asked.

Lotus gave a noncommittal shrug.

They were in the forest, where Matreen had sentry duty while the village meeting was taking place. Lotus could have optioned to stay back at the house with the younger children (the eldest of whom was thirteen), but had decided that it might be worthwhile to stand guard with Matreen instead.

As to her question, Lotus was really in a poor position to respond. Frankly speaking, he was a stranger here, and didn't know enough about his surroundings to make an assessment, and he admitted as much.

"Your surroundings?" Matreen said, sounding incredulous. Then she pointed in various directions, saying in exasperation, "That way is the river, there's the village square, that's to my home."

"It's not 'surroundings' in that sense — I'm fine with directions," Lotus said defensively. "What I mean is that I'm not familiar enough with things here to be able to differentiate natural sounds from unnatural ones. In short, I don't know what to listen for."

Despite his explanation, Matreen just continued to look at him like he was a useless sack of rotten potatoes that she was being asked to eat.

"I find it hard to believe my father thinks *you* will fulfill this prophecy," she finally said.

"Well, I'm certainly not laying claim to it, if that's what you're wondering," Lotus said. "Maybe your father sees something that neither of us do."

"I know what I saw — you almost drowning in the river, almost getting washed away, and almost getting captured by Sentinels. An auspicious start for a prophesied deliverer."

"Hold on," Lotus said, a little miffed. "I just said that—"

Suddenly alert, Matreen made a curt gesture with her hand, cutting him off in mid-sentence as she ducked down low. Lotus followed her example. He still hadn't really heard or seen anything that would make him wary, but he did feel a certain amount of tension building in the air.

After tapping his shoulder to get his attention, Matreen pointed. There, about a hundred yards away, he spied something moving through the trees. After a moment, he realized what it was: an airboat, similar to the one he had seen on the river. As he watched, he noticed that it was headed in their direction, with a Sentinel guard and an Enforcer on board.

Matreen grabbed his hand and, staying low, headed to a nearby tree that was exceptionally large — maybe eight feet in diameter at the base. Once there, they hunkered down, trying to stay out of sight. Releasing his hand, Matreen let out a soft sigh of relief.

After a few seconds, she inched towards the side of the tree and ventured a glance around it. Almost immediately, Lotus saw her tense up and understood what she must be seeing.

She slid back into hiding and whispered, "It's headed this way."

Instinctively, Lotus did a quick assessment and realized that they were at a distinct disadvantage. They had no weapons or armor, and thus lacked any offensive or defensive capability. Their best option seemed to be staying hidden.

Matreen evidently came to the same conclusion, because — after peeking around the tree once again — she began backing up slowly and gesturing for Lotus to do the same. As the front of the airboat became visible to them, they covertly crept backwards, using the radial shape of the bole of the tree to stay out of sight.

Their plan seemed to work. As the airboat went past their hiding spot, Lotus leaned around Matreen and saw the guard on board with his back to them, standing alone in the interior of the vehicle. The man didn't seem to have noticed them, which should have been cause for celebration. Instead, something about the situation nagged at Lotus' brain for a few seconds, and then it came to him like a bolt from the blue.

Alone?! Lotus shouted to himself. *Where was the—*

Klaxons going off in his brain, Lotus spun to his rear defensively without finishing his train of thought — only to find himself immediately snatched off the ground and then slammed into the tree that had been their hiding place hard enough to knock bark off the thing.

As he slid to the ground, everything went dark.

Chapter 14

Lotus came to with the sounds of a struggle and pleas for help ringing in his ears. His vision was hazy for a second, and then — as it came into focus — he saw Matreen being manhandled by the guard, who was attempting to drag her into the airboat. The Enforcer stood nearby. For a second, Lotus wondered why it wasn't helping get Matreen into the vehicle, and then he understood: the guard was enjoying his tussle with her.

Lotus' head swam as he got to his feet; apparently he had only been out for a few seconds. Wobbling slightly, he began running towards the airboat.

He wasn't particularly quiet in his approach, but neither the guard nor the Enforcer seemed to notice him. That changed, however, when Lotus got within a dozen paces of them. At that juncture, the Enforcer, perhaps hearing something, turned in his direction just as Lotus was leaping from the ground.

He planted both feet in the Enforcer's midsection, but he would have had done better to kick a brick wall. The Enforcer didn't budge an inch; Lotus, on the other hand, fell immediately and painfully to the ground.

The Enforcer reached down and grabbed Lotus by the neck with one hand. It lifted him off the ground, and then began to squeeze.

Lotus felt as though his neck was going to snap off. More importantly, he couldn't get any air. He brought both hands up and tried to tear the giant's grip away. He'd have had more luck hammering a nail into wood with his eyeball. The Enforcer's hand didn't move an inch.

Starting to see spots before his eyes, Lotus beat and kicked at the hand holding him, despite knowing how ineffectual it was. As his vision started to go dark, he began to panic. He would have screamed if he'd had any air in his lungs. Instead, all he could do was shout inside his own skull.

Let me go!!! he screamed mentally.

And just like that, the Enforcer's grip loosened, at least enough for Lotus to get in a few desperate breaths of air. Not sure what was happening (but willing to take what he could get), he mentally shouted again for the Enforcer to release him. This time, it opened up its fingers and Lotus slipped to the ground, wheezing.

"Let's go," said the guard, who now had Matreen in the airboat (and probably thought Lotus was either dead or dying).

The Enforcer seemed to hesitate for a moment, then climbed into the waiting vehicle. Lotus reached for it feebly, but it zoomed away and was out of sight within seconds.

Chapter 15

Lotus ran towards the village square at top speed. It had taken him a few minutes to recover from being throttled, at which time chasing after the airboat — even if he'd known how to track it — would have been pointless. There was no way he could match its speed. The only thing he could think to do was to tell Matreen's parents what had happened as soon as possible.

He didn't have any trouble finding the place. It was in the direction that Matreen had indicated — a group of about a dozen buildings located relatively close to each other in a clearing.

Chest heaving, Lotus was completely winded by the time he arrived. Taking a moment to gather his thoughts and catch his breath, he spied something he hadn't noticed initially: one of the Sentinel airboats. Unoccupied, it was floating next to one of the buildings that was near the center of town.

Now cautious, Lotus looked around for a weapon but could find nothing except a loose, palm-sized stone on the ground. It wasn't much, but it was better than nothing. He then began creeping cautiously towards the area in the center of the buildings, which he assumed to be the village square.

As he drew closer, Lotus could hear someone speaking but couldn't make out the words. He also kept the airboat in sight in case one of the Sentinels should come back to it. Finally, he was close enough to peek around a corner and was surprised by what he saw.

There were a few hundred people in the village square. They all seemed to be gathered around a small dais located pretty much in the center of town. Standing atop of it was a man who was speaking, and this was what had caught Lotus by surprise: the man was a Sentinel.

Lotus must have inadvertently made some noise, because one of the villagers glanced in his direction. He felt a slight moment of panic thinking that he was about to be called out in some way, but the villager turned his attention back to the Sentinel without a word. Lotus then felt rather foolish as he realized that all of his furtive sneaking around since reaching the village square was unnecessary. In his current attire, he'd fit right in. With that thought in mind, he walked out casually and joined the crowd.

" —sary," the Sentinel was saying. "As usual, we will expect full compliance."

"But that's not fair!" someone near the front shouted. "You've already taken oblations from us four times this season! Traditionally it's no more than two! Now you want more?!"

"We all do our part," the Sentinel guard said calmly. "The Dark Foe would like nothing more than for us to diminish our efforts — especially with war looming on the horizon."

"But it's too much!" said a woman near the middle of the crowd. "At this rate, there'll soon be no one left in any of the villages."

Lotus, threading his way through the crowd to the front, heard many murmur in agreement with this last speaker.

The Sentinel refused to back down, saying, "The Great Infinity guards you all, covers you with a shroud of protection. The contributions required of you are minimal in comparison."

Someone else in the crowd began to speak, but Thoban cut them off, stating "Enough!" He turned to the Sentinel. "Give us the names of who you're here for."

"There's no need," the guard replied. "We've already collected them."

Wild chatter broke out immediately amongst those gathered. Thoban spent a few moments shushing the crowd, and then faced the guard once more.

"What do you mean you already have them?" he asked.

The Sentinel smiled slyly. "We picked them up in the forest and other places surrounding your village. The sentries you had posted."

There was a harsh cry of heartbreak from the front of the crowd, close to where Lotus now found himself. It had come from Matreen's mother, Leva.

"No!" barked Norel as his wife leaned on him for support. "You can't!"

"As I said, we already have," replied the guard. "These 'sentries' were obviously surplusage of some sort since, instead of engaging in typical village occupations, they were essentially standing guard. You should thank us for taking the extra baggage off your hands. Unless, of course, there was a need for them to be out there, and this village actually has something of value that requires such vigilance."

There was silence for a moment and then, quite unexpectedly, Norel charged the Sentinel. The guard (who was younger, bigger, and stronger) was apparently ready for something like this. He let Norel get close and then, after grabbing the older man's shirt, twisted and slammed him to the ground.

While Norel lay there groaning in obvious pain, the guard pulled his gun out.

Pointing the weapon at the prone form of Norel, he said, "Attacking one of Infinity's Sentinels is a crime punishable by death."

As the guard was in the act of pulling the trigger, Lotus threw the stone he had picked up. It hit the guard's gun hand, knocking the weapon away just as it was fired. The ground near Norel's head was blasted, causing Norel to roll away slightly and put his hand up to his face for protection. The gun itself hit the ground a few feet away.

"Who dares?!" screeched the guard, looking around furiously and pulling something like a dirk from a sheath at his waist.

No one pointed Lotus out to him, but they didn't have to; the crowd immediately parted to either side of him, making it clear to the guard who the culprit was.

The guard used the dirk to point at Lotus. "You're dead."

The Sentinel advanced on Lotus, his face a mask of barely contained fury. He swung at Lotus in a cutting motion, making a wide arc with the blade. Lotus leaned back, dodging the blow, but as he leaned forward again, the guard swung the blade back towards him.

This time, Lotus didn't dodge. Instead, he caught the wrist of the hand holding the knife and gave it a hard twist. The guard squealed in pain and let go of the knife. Lotus caught it before it hit the ground, and then stabbed at the exposed area under the guard's arm, striking in a downward manner and driving the blade in to the hilt.

The guard screamed, and at the same time there was a collective gasp from the crowd. Lotus released the Sentinel's wrist, and he collapsed to the ground, dead.

Thoban looked at Lotus in shock, as did all the villagers. "What have you done?!" he demanded.

"Saved Norel's life," Lotus replied.

"No," Thoban said, shaking his head. "You've killed us all. They'll burn the village for this, drag us from our homes in the middle of the night."

"He was only trying to help," said Leva, helping her husband to his feet. "You heard what the guard said. They've already taken more of us. This was bound to happen sooner or later."

"You ignorant *zheisten*!" Thoban shouted, using a term that put Lotus in mind of a domesticated animal like a cow. "We don't even know if he was telling the truth."

"It's true," Lotus said. "I was with Matreen when they took her. That's why I'm here. I ran to tell you as soon as I could."

Leva started to cry, burying her head in her husband's shoulder. Norel, clearly trying to be strong for his wife, was fighting back tears himself.

"Thoban," said one of the men nearby, "what are we going to do?"

"We have to contact the Sentinels and tell them what happened," Thoban replied. "Basically, a stranger came to town and killed the guard. But not before the guard killed him as well."

It took a moment for the words to sink in, for Lotus to understand what was being implied.

"What?!" he yelled.

"I'm sorry, but it's the only way," Thoban said, drawing a wicked-looking knife from behind his back. "The Sentinels will want blood for the death of one of their own. This way, we give it to them." Speaking to the crowd in general, he then said, "Hold him."

A few hands began reaching for Lotus, timidly at first; he slapped them away, following a few up with punches if the person's face was in range. All the while, he tried to keep Thoban and his blade at least on the periphery of his vision.

"I said grab him, you fools!" Thoban grumbled. Having seen what had happened to the guard, he was apparently in no rush to close with Lotus himself.

At Thoban's urging, more people seemed intent on getting their hands on Lotus. However, after a few kicks and punches, they collectively decided on a different tactic: they surrounded him, although none were bold enough to charge directly at him. Instead, they gave him a wide berth and began shouting, trying to taunt him.

Although not bothered in the least by the jeering, Lotus felt a pressing need to get away from this growing mob; it was only a matter of time before someone got their hands on a sickle, a shovel, or something with some reach that could possibly counter his martial skills

Without warning, a trio of fellows, egging one another on, came at him at once. One dove at his legs, wrapping them up, while the other two came in on the sides.

Lotus fought to maintain his balance and stay on his feet. He was dead if he hit the ground; this crowd would tear him apart. This gave the two coming in on the sides an opportunity to grab his arms.

Lotus yanked one leg free and stomped down on the arm of the guy at his feet — right on the elbow, where the joint was touching the ground. The man screamed as the bone there was crushed, and loosened his grip on Lotus' legs.

Lotus yanked his right arm towards his left side, pulling the fellow holding it in close. At the same time, he lowered his head and plowed it into the man's face. He heard the satisfying crack of bone and when he looked up, the man on his right was blinking, clearly unable to focus his vision. The fellow brought his hands up protectively towards what was plainly a broken nose that was gushing blood. Lotus backhanded him, sending the man stumbling back into the crowd.

His right hand now free, Lotus drove it into the stomach of the man holding his left arm. The man let go of Lotus and doubled over in pain. Lotus gave him an uppercut that lifted him off his feet.

Alarm bells started going off in Lotus mind, and a second later he realized why.

Thoban! He had lost track of the village councilor (and the knife he was wielding).

Instinctively, Lotus spun around — just as Thoban struck. The councilor had apparently been attempting to stab Lotus in the back, but with his anticipated victim now facing him, the knife looked as though it would penetrate Lotus' chest instead. However, rather than the blade going in, there was the distinctive clang of metal on metal as the knife failed to penetrate. Although surprised, Thoban displayed faster-than-expected reflexes, trying to slice with the knife before leaping back out of reach. But, as with his attempt at stabbing, there was no discernable effect.

Apparently tired of waiting for others to do his dirty work for him, Thoban began circling, knife at the ready. Lotus turned to face the councilor from the side, presenting him with the smallest possible target; he rocked back and forth on the balls of his feet, attempting to stay agile.

All of a sudden, Thoban's eyes bulged, becoming even larger than they had when Lotus had killed the guard. The councilor flung down his blade, dropped to his knees and lowered his head.

Lotus, wondering if this was some new stealth strategy, spun around. There was no one behind him. However, there was another collective gasp from the crowd behind him, and almost in unison they went down to their knees as well. Lotus slowly turned in a circle, and as he did, the rest of the crowd also knelt down before him.

What the hell is going on? he thought. He started to look himself over, wondering what was happening, and then he saw what the issue was.

Thoban hadn't been able to stab Lotus in the chest because apparently the knife had struck the pendant Lotus was wearing. Even more, when the councilor had sliced at Lotus, he had cut open the tunic, making a hole that the pendant slipped through a few moments later, thereby becoming visible to the crowd. It was because of the pendant that the villagers were all kneeling.

The pendant Lotus always wore.

The pendant that wouldn't come off.

The pendant that marked him as a member of the Royal House of Eon.

Chapter 16

"A-a-apologies, my liege," said Thoban. "W-we didn't know who you were. We only… We only wanted to protect ourselves."

Lotus lifted his pendant slightly. "You recognize this?"

Thoban nodded. "Yes, milord. It brands you as one of the Highborn, a member of the ruling elite."

"Yes," said Lotus, thankful that this gift from his father had once again saved his life. "I am indeed a member of the Royal House — the eldest son of Eon the Golden."

It felt awkward to Lotus to say these things. While true, it was information that he had only recently discovered, and it struck him as weird to describe himself in such lofty terms. Still, if it would keep this mob from laying hands on him again, he'd take it.

That said, the crowd in question had a weird reaction to his last statement. Several women fainted outright. Many of those kneeling began exchanging odd glances with one another, and a low murmuring began spreading through the throngs gathered around him. Moreover, the tone sounded slightly menacing.

Lotus didn't like this particular shift in the wind.

Best to do something about it now, while I still have some semblance of authority, he thought.

"This assembly is over," he announced loudly. "All of you, go home. Now."

A few more glances were exchanged among those gathered, and for a moment he thought the crowd wasn't going to obey.

"As you wish," said Thoban, rising to his feet. Following his lead, the others stood as well, and the crowd began to disperse, although they all stayed well back from Lotus (and a few seemed to give him the stink eye).

"Leva. Norel," Lotus said. "Not you two. Stay."

The couple, who had been kneeling as well, looked nervously at each other but complied with his request. In a few minutes, the three of them were alone.

"Okay," Lotus said, "tell me what the hell that was all about. One second they're kissing my ass, the next they're looking like they want to string me up by my balls."

"Please, liege," Norel began. "We apologi—"

"Stop with the 'liege' shit!" Lotus said adamantly, making Leva flinch. "I'm the same guy who took a shower in your house earlier today. I ran all the way here to tell you what happened to Matreen, and ended up almost getting killed for it."

"Is it true?" Norel asked timidly. "Are you truly…*his* son?"

"Who, Eon?" Lotus said. "Yes, and if I can use that fact to save Matreen I will, but I need to know what's going on."

"Then you truly don't understand what it is that you've said," said Leva. "Or what it means."

"Obviously not," Lotus replied. "If I did, I wouldn't be begging you to explain it to me."

Leva and Norel exchanged a glance.

"Do you really think you can save our daughter?" Norel asked.

"If I can, I will," Lotus replied in the sincerest tone he could muster. "I promise you."

Norel looked at his wife.

"Please, Norel," she said pleadingly. "I can't lose another. I just can't."

She leaned against him and started crying again.

"Very well," Norel said, and then turned to Lotus. "You wish to know why the villagers' assessment of you suddenly changed from awe and respect to fear and loathing."

Lotus nodded. "Yes."

Norel took a deep breath. "Because the one you mentioned, the one you named as your father — he's the Dark Foe."

Chapter 17

"That's not possible," Lotus said softly. He knew his father could be harsh under certain circumstances, but he hadn't seen anything on a scale which suggested that Eon could be considered this "Dark Foe" he'd heard mentioned several times.

"But it is," said Norel. "That is the name of Infinity's great enemy."

"Aren't you guys planning a rebellion against Infinity anyway?" Lotus asked. "Haven't you ever heard that the enemy of my enemy is my friend? If my father is so great an antagonist that Infinity won't let his name be spoken, shouldn't all you rebels be lining up to beg for his support?"

"It's one thing to seek a better regime," Leva said. "It is quite another to align yourselves with an enemy who has tried to destroy your people."

"I find it hard to believe Eon would ever do that," Lotus said. "Is this something that you have personal knowledge of, or just stories that have been spread by Infinity?"

"It is our history," Norel declared. Then he added, "As dictated by Infinity."

"Wait a minute," Lotus said, as something occurred to him. "When everyone saw my pendant, they recognized it as a symbol of a Highborn, but thought I was part of the Royal House here, in the Infinituum."

"Correct," said Leva. She pointed to his pendant — more specifically, to an image of a sunburst emblazoned on it. "We recognize this sigil of the royal family."

Lotus scratched his temple in thought. "So the same image that designates royalty in my father's continuum is indicative of the same thing here. Does that mean… Are Eon and Infinity related?"

"They are siblings," Norel replied. "Twins."

Chapter 18

Lotus rubbed his temples as he sought to process what he'd just heard. A million other questions popped up in his brain, but Norel spoke before he could ask any of them.

"You should leave now," Norel told him. "You won't have much time."

"What do you mean?" asked Lotus.

Norel gave him a look of incredulity. "Are you a fool? You are the son of the Dark Foe. Word will spread quickly to the capital city — to Infinity — that you are in our village."

"So I need to find a place to hide out," Lotus said. "Is there a rebel camp, or…" He trailed off.

"No, there's no such camp," Leva assured him. "And even if there were, they wouldn't accept you once they found out who you were — who your father is. As far as they're concerned, you're the son of wickedness personified."

"Let's think, Leva," her husband said. "There must be some place he can go where they can't find him."

Leva shook her head. "This is the Infinituum. Infinity rules supreme here. There's no place where they can't find him."

"Well, how about the place they're least likely to look?" Lotus asked, giving them a sly smile.

****

"You're mad," declared Norel as Lotus dumped the body of the guard he'd killed into the airboat, which was still near the village square. "Completely mad."

"If you have a better idea, I'm all ears," said Lotus. "Besides, you want me to rescue Matreen, and this is the only way I'll even come close to doing that."

Norel said nothing; he merely looked at his wife, who nodded.

"I'll help you as much as I can, for my daughter's sake," he said. "Despite the fact that you're the spawn of evil."

Lotus rolled his eyes in exasperation, but said nothing.

Chapter 19

As the airboat sped towards the capital city, Lotus — dressed in the uniform of the Sentinel he had killed — had to admit that Norel was right to a certain extent. This was an insane plan. He was practically delivering himself to Infinity, who — if Matreen's parents were correct — would be sending patrols out all over the place to find him. But that was the beauty of his plan. The last place anyone would expect him to be was practically under the same roof with the people who would be hunting him.

He wasn't that familiar with the airboat controls, but fortunately, Norel knew how to program the autopilot. Following Lotus' instructions, Norel had ordered the boat to first travel along a path *away* from the capital (to thereby confuse any villagers who might have reported Lotus' movements), and then it would make a long, circuitous arc and head back to the capital.

"Once there, you're on your own," Norel had told him. "We have no advice for you beyond that point, because no villager taken there has ever returned."

Lotus had nodded in understanding, and then gotten underway.

During the course of the trip, since he wasn't actually piloting, he had stripped the dead guard of his uniform and then dumped the body overboard. The outfit had blood on it, but he dipped it into a lake that the airboat flew over at one point and then spent a fair amount of time cleaning it as best he could. By the time the capital came into view, he was wearing his new garb. It wasn't a perfect fit and he wasn't likely to pass inspection at a military parade, but it would probably pass muster if someone did little more than just glance at him.

His first view of the capital as he drew close was mesmerizing. It was massive in scope, seeming to stretch from one end of the horizon to the other, with towers reaching high into the sky. Based solely on size, it had to be a megalopolis, at the very least.

The airboat's autopilot guided his vehicle toward the western portion of the city. As he drew closer, the city seemed to grow exponentially, looming over him and making him feel exceedingly small.

The boat headed to a massive building that resembled a giant warehouse. Looking around, Lotus saw other boats arriving, as well as quite a few that were leaving. He got the distinct impression that Sentinels worked around the clock.

His vehicle entered the warehouse through a massive hangar door that was open. Inside, the place appeared to be something of a giant parking lot, with airboats sitting motionless in various designated spots. The airboat Lotus was in automatically headed towards an empty space and, once there, seemed to power down. Various other vehicles were arriving at the same time, with the occupants getting out and heading towards a central area near the back of the warehouse. Not wanting to appear conspicuous, Lotus began walking in the same direction.

As he marched along, Lotus noted that a number of the Sentinels seemed to have been accompanied by Enforcers while they were out. He sent up a silent prayer of thanks that the guard he'd killed had been alone — otherwise the outcome of their fight might have ended very differently.

At the back of the warehouse, the guards passed through a door and into another building. At that juncture, they seemed to go in different directions. Those with oblations headed down a corridor to the right, while those who hadn't brought back tribute of some sort went down a hallway to the left (to an area that Lotus later learned was essentially a locker room for washing up and changing clothes). Although he didn't have an oblation of any type, Lotus followed the guards heading right.

The hallway in that direction terminated in a room where a young guard wearing an earpiece and holding something like a computer tablet seemed to be cataloging the oblations as they were brought in, taking pertinent information such as the name of each person, the village or town they were from, etc. Thus, most of the Sentinels found themselves waiting in line with the oblations they had brought.

Lotus casually walked to the front of the line, looking for Matreen while at the same time trying not to arouse suspicion that he wasn't where he was supposed to be. As he suspected, Matreen was not there. Of course, she had left hours before him, so she had probably already been processed through the system here. Unsure of what to do, Lotus sort of meandered back and forth — going from the front of the line to the end and back again — while slowly putting together a plan of action.

After about fifteen minutes, he saw the young guard with the tablet get replaced by a colleague with similar equipment. The initial guard then turned and headed in the direction of a narrow doorway. Lotus hurried to catch up, following behind him.

****

Lotus trailed his quarry for maybe twenty minutes, at which point the guard stopped in front of what appeared to be a locked door with a glass window in it. Grabbing a card attached to his waist by an extendable line and a clip, the guard swiped it across what turned out to be a scanner of some sort set in the wall. A moment later, there was an audible click and the door unlocked. The guard went inside.

Careful to avoid attention, Lotus crept to the door and peeked in through the window. There, he saw the young guard sitting in front of a computer monitor. The fellow had attached the laptop to the monitor, and was presumably downloading all of the information he had gathered thus far.

Lotus watched him for a few minutes, the rudiments of a plan starting to take shape in his mind. He stepped away from the door and then tried to keep from appearing completely idle while waiting for the guard to come out of the room. A short time later, his patience was rewarded when the guy exited. He glanced at Lotus, eyes narrowed slightly in suspicion as he put a hand up to his earpiece, then began walking in the opposite direction.

Lotus followed him, concentrating intently on the card at the guard's waist. After a few moments, the clip holding it in place seemed to undo itself, and the card fell to the floor. The guard kept walking, not seeming to notice; Lotus practically pounced on his prize, retrieving the card and then racing back to the locked room. He swiped the card across the scanner and entered.

He found himself in a modest-sized room, maybe ten-by-ten feet in size. He headed to the computer monitor that the guard had been sitting at before. The screen, initially dark, must have somehow sensed his presence because it suddenly blazed to life, displaying a weird interplay of colors and symbols.

After a few moments of experimentation, he realized that the monitor was a touchscreen. It also became apparent that it was waiting for him to do something. Then he noticed, on the side of the monitor, a smaller version of the scanner that had been on the door. He swiped the card across it, and the colors and symbols on the screen appeared to rearrange themselves, with a number of characters flashing in blue suddenly becoming the most prominent items on the display.

As before, the computer system seemed to be waiting for him to do something — probably in relation to the glowing symbols. Unfortunately, he had no idea what the characters represented.

Lotus sighed in exasperation. Evidently, although his father had implanted knowledge of his people's spoken language in Lotus' head, he had failed to also transfer understanding of the written word. In short, with respect to Eon's language, Lotus was illiterate. (He decided then and there that he would at least be a *functioning* illiterate, but he was still illiterate nonetheless.)

Lotus thought for a second, and then said in a firm tone, "Go to audible mode." When the computer didn't respond, he tried again, using various word combinations. "Enable voice authorization. Voice command. Verbal command."

"Switching to verbal command mode," said an androgynous voice that came from the monitor, making Lotus almost want to cheer. "Please initiate verbal authorization."

The machine's last statement brought a quick end to Lotus' euphoria over establishing verbal control. He thought for a moment, trying to figure out how to give the computer what it wanted. While he was studying the problem, the computer again requested that he initiate verbal authorization.

Unable to come up with anything, Lotus decided to try the direct approach. "How do I ini—"

"Voice scan in progress," the computer declared, not letting Lotus finish his question. Apparently it had simply been waiting for him to speak. However, if it was analyzing his voice, there was no way this was going to end well.

As if in confirmation of Lotus' conclusion, a few seconds later the computer stated, "Unable to verify voice pattern. Initiating biometric scan."

Before Lotus could react, a light shined on him from above, bathing him in a harsh red glow for a second. His mind was racing, trying to come up with options. A voice scan was bad enough, but there was no way he was passing a bio-scan; his physiology, as he understood it, was radically different internally from both normal humans and his father's people. The question, however, was what would the computer do when he failed this particular test.

The answer was received in short order, with the symbols on the monitor suddenly flashing red and the machine announcing, "Biometric data unverified. Biometric data unmatched. Biome—"

Somewhat in a panic, Lotus had been preparing to bolt when the computer suddenly stopped speaking and the monitor went blank except for a glowing blue prism. Obviously something was happening. The question was whether Lotus could risk sticking around to find out what it was. Flipping a mental coin, he decided to stay where he was.

He sat there, nervously tapping a foot on the floor as he waited to see what the computer's next move would be. Finally, after what seemed like forever (but was surely no more than a minute), a sunburst like the one on Lotus' pendant appeared on the screen and the computer voice said, "Royal sigil recognized. How may we serve you, sire?"

Lotus let out a sigh of relief.

Chapter 20

The computer, having noted Lotus' pendant when it scanned him, was keenly responsive to his questions. It quickly became evident that, because of his royal standing, no information seemed to be off-limits or unauthorized. Basically, nothing was above his pay grade.

He quickly got it to focus on the recent oblations brought to the city — in particular, adolescent females. He kept trying to narrow the focus down by giving more info — village size, proximity to major geographical features (like rivers) — when the computer, through various hints, made it clear to him that he could search for a specific person by name. (Apparently the law provided for regular updating of census records.)

Once he gave the entire name of Matreen bao-Negoy, the computer informed him (as well as showed him on the monitor) that she was being held in some sort of cellblock not far from where the airboat hangar was. That was the easy part; what was trickier was coming up with an escape plan. After thinking about it for a few minutes, he hit upon a thought that could possibly solve the problem.

"Computer," Lotus began, "what are the limits of my authority?"

The response was immediate and gratifying. "No such parameters are established for Highborn."

"So if I wished to question a prisoner in private, it would be allowed?"

"Affirmative, although confirmation of authority or identity would be required."

"And how can those be established?"

"Voice pattern and biometric data can be entered into the security network. If such is your desire, I can do so now."

"Hmmm. Does that data have to be tied to my identity?"

"Question vague. Please rephrase."

"In order for me to exercise my authority, do I have to reveal that I'm royalty?"

"Negative. Authority can be linked to voice pattern and biometrics without the necessity of personal identification."

"Okay, then do it."

There was silence for a moment, and then the computer said, "Requested linkage complete."

"Thank you."

There was another brief pause, during which the computer seemed to be processing information, and then it said, "You're welcome." The act intrigued Lotus, but he decided he'd come back to it later. At the moment, he needed to rescue Matreen.

He started to rise, thinking how happy Matreen's parents would be if he could get her out. She'd probably become a legend — the first oblation to ever return from the city. And on the heels of that thought came another series of questions. Lotus sat back down.

"New question," he began. "What becomes of the oblations — the people — who are brought to the city?"

"They are put into the service of the Great Infinity."

"Yes, but in what manner?"

"Some are sent to retrieve valuable ore and minerals…" The monitor showed an image of an underground cavern, with men and women hard at work mining in what looked like brutal conditions.

"Others are involved in the testing of new technology..." The image changed, basically showing someone being used as a living crash-test dummy for a high-powered rocket of some sort.

"A number are given the privilege of serving as domestics..." The scene changed once again, showing individuals being forced to serve, clean, cook, and so on.

The computer went on, describing the different ways in which oblations were put to use and showing accompanying images; Lotus basically tuned the rest of it out. No matter the spin the computer offered, there was really only one term to describe what he was being shown: slave labor.

Out of curiosity, Lotus asked, "Matreen bao-Negoy. What manner of service is she expected to offer?"

He feared the response he would get. Being a pretty young girl, there were all kinds of degrading and dehumanizing things she could be subjected to, and — based on what he'd seen thus far — he didn't think any of it beyond what the laws of this place would allow. The answer he got, however, was far worse than he could have imagined.

"Matreen bao-Negoy is slated for bio-modulation, reconfiguration, and repurposing," the computer said.

Lotus frowned. "What the fuck does that mean?"

In response, the computer began offering an explanation, but it never fully registered with Lotus. Instead, his attention was captured by the accompanying display on the monitor. It initially showed a nude woman, and then shifted through a series of gruesome images which depicted — through surgery, bizarre treatments, and some sort of unknown body-morphing — the transformation of the female from a person into an Enforcer.

Lotus felt like he wanted to vomit.

His mouth dry, Lotus asked, "Are all Enforcers women?"

"Although masculine in appearance, Enforcers are gender-neutral," the computer responded. At the same time, the image on the monitor changed to show an unclothed Enforcer. As the computer had indicated, it lacked genitalia.

Lotus shook his head. "No. I mean are they all created from females?"

"Negative. The vast majority of Enforcers created from repurposed stock are derived from males."

The computer's phrasing struck Lotus as odd, making him ask a follow-up question. "Is there another method of creating Enforcers, aside from what you've shown me?"

"Affirmative. Traditionally, Enforcers were constructed from synthetic bio-stock rather than natural organic material."

In conjunction with this statement, the monitor showed an Enforcer floating in a liquid-filled tank in some kind of lab.

"What is the reason for the change in methodology for the creation of Enforcers?"

"The methodology has *not* changed. An *additional* method has been developed."

"Then state the reason for the additional method."

"The original technique did not produce Enforcers quickly enough to suit the Great Infinity, who requires them for the upcoming war with the Dark Foe."

"Hold on," Lotus said, thinking. "Infinity's building an army of Enforcers?"

"Affirmative."

The monitor screen now shifted to show some type of massive storage facility, which was filled with nothing but Enforcers all standing shoulder to shoulder.

Lotus stared, not quite believing what he was seeing. In Eon's continuum, Enforcers were essentially used as individually assigned protectors for the Highborn. To the best of his knowledge, they had never been produced on a massive scale as Infinity had done. One of the damn things was capable of taking on a regiment of soldiers. An army of them would be unstoppable.

Lotus had more questions, but he couldn't stay in here forever — he had to get to Matreen. Still, he was loath to leave with so much information at his fingertips. Maybe there was a way…

"Computer, is there a way to make you mobile?" Lotus asked.

"I am not housed on a single platform. My programming is running simultaneously on a multitude of hardware devices, making it impractical to—"

"No," Lotus said, interrupting. "What I really meant to ask is if there's a way I can stay in contact with you once I leave this room?"

"If you are willing to wear it, an earpiece can allow us to stay in communication."

"That sounds fine. Where can I get one?"

"On the table to your right."

Lotus looked where instructed and saw a table that he had observed upon entering the room but hadn't taken particular note of. On the table was a glass display case, in which were several earpieces and a couple of computer tablets like that of the guard Lotus had swiped the access card from. He stalked over to the case, opened it, and took out one of the earpieces.

It was slightly heavier than he anticipated, and based on what he could see from a cursory examination, it seemed to have a fair amount of complex circuitry inside.

He took a moment to fit it in his ear, and then — after also snagging one of the tablets — said, "Can you hear me?"

"Yes," the computer answered in his ear.

"Great," Lotus said with a smile. "We're in business."

Chapter 21

With the computer giving him directions, Lotus was able to find where Matreen was being held in almost no time. Moreover, the guards in that area gave him no trouble after he said he wanted to speak to one of the prisoners alone. They merely verified his authorization via voice pattern, and then showed him to what Lotus would have described as an interrogation room. A few minutes later, Matreen was brought in.

At first she didn't appear to recognize him. She seemingly took one look at his attire and just assumed he was a Sentinel. It wasn't until he smiled at her that she seemed to take note of his features. Her eyes went wide, and then she raced to him and gave him a hug.

"I can't believe it!" she exclaimed, stepping back. "What are you doing here?"

"Rescuing you, of course!" he replied.

"But how…how is this possible?"

Lotus sighed. "It's a long story, but we don't have time for that now. We have to—"

Lotus stopped speaking as the door to the cell was abruptly thrown open. In marched three Sentinels — two younger guards with their weapons at the ready, and one who appeared to be the older, ranking officer.

"What's this?" the senior officer asked.

"An interrogation," Lotus replied.

"Really?" the man said. "I would have sworn it was more like a reunion."

"A reunion?" Lotus repeated.

Rather than respond directly, the officer said, "Computer, play back recording of this room from the time the female entered."

Recording? Lotus thought. He wanted to kick himself. He should have realized that, if this were an interrogation room, the events in it would be recorded.

"Complying," said a voice that Lotus recognized as the computer.

A holographic scene suddenly came to life before those in the room. It showed, as had been requested, what had happened once Matreen entered the room.

"Freeze image," the officer said just as the hologram showed Matreen giving Lotus a hug. "As I said, it seems to be a reunion."

Lotus, who had been thinking furiously for the past few seconds, had hit upon an idea that probably wouldn't work but was all he had at his disposal.

"How dare you," Lotus said, frowning angrily. "How dare you?!"

"Wh-what?" said the officer, suddenly looking unsure of himself.

"This woman is one of our agents," Lotus stated, pointing to Matreen. "Her job is to infiltrate the villages and provide us with information concerning possible dissenters. There have been reports of a rebellion brewing."

"Rebellion?" the man said. "There have been rumors…"

"Well, the Great Infinity wants facts, not rumors, and you have chosen to interfere with our investigation, forcing me to reveal what should have remained confidential."

"N-n-no. I only meant to confirm that nothing untoward was happening."

"Understandable," Lotus said, "but I don't know how I can avoid reporting this."

The officer turned to the two guards who had accompanied him. "Leave us." A moment later, they were gone.

"Please," the officer said pleadingly. "There's no need to make a report. There must be something I can do to make up for my misstep."

Lotus looked at the man as if weighing some decision, and then let out a deep breath. "Very well. I understand that you were only trying to protect the interests of the Great Infinity, so you shouldn't be punished for that. If I have your word that you — and your two underlings — won't tell anyone about this, I can avoid reporting it."

"Thank you!" the man said, clearly relieved. "I'll make sure my men don't say anything."

"Also, I need you to erase that recording you made."

"Absolutely." The officer cleared his throat and then said, "Computer, erase all recordings of activity in this room since the first of the current occupants entered, and discontinue all such recording until otherwise instructed."

"Complying," the computer announced.

Without further ado, the officer apologized, and then beat a hasty retreat from the room. Lotus ran a hand through his hair and felt tension drain from him. That had been exceptionally close.

"Computer," he said. "Please confirm that all recordings of me and Matreen in this room have been erased and that no additional recording is taking place."

"Confirmed," the computer replied in his ear.

Lotus nodded, then rubbed his chin in thought as something occurred to him. Matreen tried to say something to him, but he shushed her.

"Computer," he said, "were you aware that events in this room were being recorded?"

"Affirmative."

The answer felt like something of a betrayal to Lotus, which was silly because this was a machine he was talking about.

"If you knew about events in here being recorded, why didn't you warn us?"

"I am essentially programmed to be reactive in nature. For instance, if asked a question, I respond. However, if no query is presented to me, I do not volunteer an answer. Being proactive is fundamentally beyond my mandate."

"So if there was a group of armed guards waiting to gun us down as soon as we stepped out of this room, you wouldn't tell us."

"That is correct."

Lotus pondered the facts for a moment. "If I ordered you to act autonomously with respect to protecting me and my interests — such as warning me if I'm in danger — could you do so?"

There was silence for a moment as the computer seemed to contemplate the appropriate response, and then it said, "If so ordered by you, I can comply, but with two restrictions."

"Which are?"

"First, if another Highborn of equal rank issues an order which countermands anything you have dictated, the net effect will be a nullity. I will not obey either and will shift back to the status quo before any of the conflicting commands were given."

"Understood," Lotus said. The situation described would be like a kid caught in the middle of an argument between Mom and Dad and being asked to decide which of them was right. "What's the second restriction?"

"Any mandate from the Great Infinity, who outranks you, will be given precedence over your commands."

Lotus wasn't really surprised by that. "Again, understood. However, can you give me notice when any such orders or commands of mine are overridden?"

"Bearing in mind the restrictions noted, I can comply."

"Excellent. Please act autonomously in the manner we have discussed."

"Complying."

"One other thing," Lotus said. "Your voice lacks distinctiveness, so in a crowded room I wouldn't know if you were speaking to me or someone else."

"You would like it changed," said the computer, anticipating where Lotus was going. "Is this better?"

Lotus blinked in surprise. The computer had spoken its last question in a honeyed, feminine voice that was completely unexpected.

"Uh....yeah," Lotus muttered. "That's, uh... That's actually quite good."

"Excuse me," Matreen said, interrupting. "If I'm allowed to speak now, can we focus on escaping from here?"

Lotus turned slightly red. In truth, he had gotten a little wrapped up in dealing with the computer, but bearing in mind what he had found out, it seemed like time well spent.

"Escaping shouldn't be that hard," Lotus said. "Assuming they're still buying my story about you being a Sentinel agent, we should be able to waltz right out of here."

"What about my brother?" Matreen asked.

"Excuse me?"

"My brother. He was taken before. Can we find him and take him with us?"

"I don't know," Lotus replied with a shrug. "Computer, can you find…" He glanced at Matreen.

"Denib bao-Negoy," she said, anxiously.

"Denib bao-Negoy," Lotus repeated. "And please respond so that my companion can hear you."

The computer answered almost immediately. "Denib bao-Negoy serves the Great Infinity as a miner. However, I would not recommend his extraction."

"Why not?" Lotus asked.

"As with most oblations, he has been outfitted with a control collar."

Lotus's brow wrinkled in confusion. "What's that?"

"A device meant to place restraints on the movements of servants," the computer replied.

Sound from the tablet he had previously taken drew his attention to the device's screen. Looking at it, with Matreen peeking over his shoulder, he saw an image of a metal collar around someone's throat. Now that it had been pointed out to him, he recalled seeing something similar on almost all the slave labor the computer had shown him earlier, although he hadn't taken particular note of it.

"If a servant goes too far from his or her designated work area," the computer continued, "an explosive in the collar is triggered."

The tablet's screen showed, in graphic detail, the result of one such bomb being activated.

That explains why no oblations are ever seen again in the old hometown, Lotus thought. He glanced at Matreen, who looked devastated; she raised a hand to her neck, as if to double-check that no such collar was attached to her. (Evidently, the new arrivals hadn't been in custody long enough for that stage of in-processing to occur.)

"Is there a way to deactivate the bomb?" Lotus asked.

"The collars are not designed to come off. Therefore, a method of deactivation was never contemplated. Nevertheless, I can attempt to devise an algorithm which will disengage the explosive, but it will take time. Moreover, I am unable to estimate the juncture at which a solution might be forthcoming."

"Please begin devising the algorithm," Lotus said. He then turned to Matreen. "I'm sorry, but we can't wait around indefinitely until the computer *possibly* comes up with a way to get your brother out of here."

Matreen bit her lip. "If we can't take Denib, what about the others?"

Lotus was nonplussed. "What others?"

"The others that they brought here. I wasn't the only one they picked up. In fact, they're out there rounding up hundreds — maybe even thousands — of people every day from all over the Infinituum."

New stock for Infinity's army, Lotus thought.

"I'm sorry," he said sincerely. "I can't do anything for them."

"But I just saw you exercise authority over a Sentinel officer."

"There's a difference between that and what you're asking. I can't do anything for the others."

Matreen shook her head defiantly. "Then you can just leave me here. There's no way I'm leaving without them."

Lotus made a sound of exasperation. "Look, I can probably get one person out, maybe two or three — the others from your village who were also picked up. But no matter how much authority the guards think I have, they aren't going to believe a large-scale version of the bullshit I was just shoveling. There's no way I'm going to convince them that every single person they picked up today is a spy for their side."

"Then we have to think of something else."

"Under other circumstances, and given an adequate amount of time, maybe we could come up with a viable plan. But right now, there's a small window of opportunity, and it's not going to stay open for very long."

The look on Matreen's face told Lotus that the reasonableness of his argument had been lost on her. He could see her drawing in a deep breath (most likely in preparation to argue with him).

However, before she could utter a word, the computer spoke; its new, feminine voice came through the room's speakers (presumably so Matreen could also hear) as it said, "Perhaps I can be of assistance."

Chapter 22

"We're ready," Lotus said. He looked at Matreen, who nodded in confirmation.

"Initiating extraction plan," the computer said.

A moment later, klaxons began going off, blasting in the interrogation room at a deafening level. In fact, the same thing should have been happening throughout that entire area.

After a few seconds, the sound of the klaxons diminished to background noise and the computer spoke in its original androgynous voice.

"Attention. Excessive levels of narxasian gas have been detected. All personnel within the following areas are advised to cease all current activity immediately and retreat to the indicated safe zones."

The computer then began to rattle off a list of various locations in the capital, including the airboat docks and the holding cells.

Listening at the door of the interrogation room, Lotus heard something like a stampede going by, accompanied by voices of barely-contained panic. After about five minutes, he took a peek outside the door; no one was in sight. He smiled as he and Matreen stepped out into the hallway.

"Which way to the holding cells?" Lotus asked.

****

In retrospect, granting the computer autonomy had been a stroke of genius. It was the computer that had come up with the current escape plan, which — Lotus had to admit — was a pretty good one. Apparently narxasian gas was some loathsome stuff and caused death in a particularly nasty way: painfully liquefying organs, with the resulting fluid seeping out through one's skin. Thus, all the computer had to do was announce that the gas was present, and a second later people were trampling one another in a mad rush for the exits. As a result, all of the areas between the holding cells and the airboats were clear. Surprisingly, however, the hardest thing about the entire rescue operation was getting the prisoners moving.

All those being held had, of course, heard the klaxons and the gas warning. Thus, when Lotus and Matreen showed up at the holding cells, many of them were loath to leave what seemed at the moment like a safe location. In fact, a number of them admittedly thought the "escape" could be a trick to deliberately expose them to the gas.

Despite much pleading, Lotus was almost completely ineffectual with respect to getting the cell occupants in motion — something he would later attribute to the fact that he was still wearing the uniform of a Sentinel. It wasn't until Matreen stepped up and began speaking that — based on the fact that she was personally known to some of the oblations (and had mutual acquaintances with others) — the cells began emptying out.

A short time later, they were at the airboats, which was where the plan got a little tricky. The computer had previously indicated its ability to purge the capital's data systems of all identifying information related to the oblations that had been brought in. In essence, it would be as though they had never been to the capital at all. In Lotus' view, however, the benefit of that would be negated if the escapees merely jumped into the first available vehicle and headed directly home. That would be a clear indication of where the oblations had initially come from.

"We need to throw any pursuing Sentinels off their trail," Lotus had said.

With that in mind, it had been decided to send out as many decoy vehicles as possible — empty airboats with preprogrammed routes. This ruse would create confusion as to where the escapees had actually gone. Moreover, any airboats that were truly used to ferry passengers were to have further instructions given to the autopilot that would take the vehicle far from where the escapees were to disembark.

It wasn't a perfect plan, but it was the best available under the circumstances. As everyone piled into the vehicles and took off, Lotus expressed aloud his hope that the mass exodus of airboats wouldn't be conspicuous. The computer assured him that it wouldn't be.

"The ingress and egress of patrols is nonstop," the computer said. "Thus, the *number* of airboats departing won't necessarily pique anyone's interest. However, the fact that so many of them are empty — and that others are filled with passengers who are more rustic than usual — would normally arouse curiosity. However, I have directed all other traffic to other hubs because of the 'gas leak,' so there is little chance of witnesses. I am also employing additional stratagems, including scrambling the GPS systems of all the airboats, so that when the vehicles are eventually recovered, there will be no way to determine where they have been."

That last part was another bit of ingenuity that Lotus was impressed with, and once again he saw the benefit of having made the computer autonomous.

The number of escapees remaining quickly dwindled. Matreen, having stayed as long as possible, was one of the last to depart.

"You should come back with me," she said to Lotus — not for the first time.

He shook his head. "I can't." He hadn't told her anything about him being the son of the Dark Foe, so she had no idea that her village was likely to give him a chilly reception if he returned. "Plus, if I leave, who's going to make sure your brother gets home?"

Matreen merely nodded in understanding and gave him a departing hug. She then climbed into the airboat waiting for her; a moment later, she was zipping away at high speed.

Chapter 23

After Matreen left, Lotus asked the computer to locate a private place for him to plot out his next move. Doing so wasn't particularly difficult; thanks to the fake gas leak, he had tons of choices. However, the longer the hoax was employed, the more likely it was to be discovered. (Of course, the jig would be up anyway once things went back to normal and it was discovered that a bunch of detainees had escaped. Therefore, it made more sense to play things out as long as possible.)

Ultimately, the computer led him to a small, unused office populated by aging furniture. He flopped down into a chair that sat in front of a small desk, and then closed his eyes, trying to think.

He spent a moment reflecting on his situation. Aside from an exhaustion-fueled sleep on a muddy riverbank, his life had been nothing but a series of crises and conflicts of late: escaping from the black ops planet; challenging the syndicate on Oasis; world-hopping with Cerulean while trying to shake Enforcers off his tail; being labeled the spawn of evil…

He could have gone on, but for some reason, his mind leaped back to his encounters with the Enforcers, who could seemingly show up at any place, at any time.

Including here, he said to himself.

And with that thought, he suddenly snapped his eyes open. In truth, the Enforcers really could pop up here, and the last thing he wanted to do was make their jobs easy for them by having his eyes closed (or worse — accidentally falling asleep). Now that he thought about it, he didn't really know the objective of the two Enforcers who had pursued him and Cerulean. He just knew that they seemed to have orders to take him alive, and wherever they'd wanted to drag him off to, his willingness to go was not a material factor. Then, as he contemplated where, exactly, the two Enforcers might have wanted to take him, a new notion occurred to him.

"Computer," he said, "where do Enforcers come from?"

"Enforcers are historically derived from synthetic—" the computer began.

"No, no, no," Lotus interjected. "I mean, what is their point of origin in space-time?"

"Originally, Enforcers were constructed in the continuum currently under the dominion of the Dark Foe. At present, they are also manufactured in the Infinituum, which exists under the auspices of the Great Infinity."

"So the only two places where they originate are this continuum and the one ruled by my fath— I mean, the Dark Foe."

Lotus felt butterflies in his stomach at the Freudian slip he'd almost made. The computer probably didn't realize he was Eon's son, and there was no telling what its reaction would be if it found out his father was the Dark Foe — especially since he'd given it autonomy.

"Affirmative," said the computer.

Sensing that the computer hadn't made the relevant connections, Lotus found himself breathing a lot easier. He turned his full attention once again to the problem of the Enforcers.

One thing he knew with almost absolute certainty was that the Enforcers that had tried to capture him were not from his father's dimension. Eon didn't have to stoop to those measures; he could have gotten Lotus to visit merely by asking.

That meant that the Enforcers in question were from *this* continuum. That also meant that Infinity was probably the person intent on his capture, although at the moment he didn't know why. Unfortunately, there was only one surefire way to find out, and that was to get the info straight from the horse's mouth.

Lotus cleared his throat and then said, "Computer, where does Infinity reside?"

"The Great Infinity's residence is a castle in the heart of the capital," the computer said. The tablet, which Lotus had placed on the table, began to show an image of a palatial estate.

"Can you tell me exactly where Infinity is at this moment?"

"For security reasons, my programming will not allow me to divulge the exact location of the Great Infinity."

"Great," Lotus mumbled sarcastically. "Just great."

"I cannot tell you where the Great Infinity is," the computer said after a moment.

"I heard you the first time."

There was a slight pause, and then the computer declared, "I cannot pinpoint for you the exact location of the Great Infinity."

Lotus frowned. "Computer, can you self-diagnose?"

"Affirmative."

"Then tell me, are you malfunctioning?"

"Negative."

"Then you are aware that you have essentially repeated the same information to me three times."

"Affirmative."

Brow furrowed in thought, Lotus tried to make sense of the computer's actions. There didn't seem to be any logic behind it, unless... Was the computer attempting to help him in some way? He decided to try something.

"Computer," he said, trying to choose his words with care, "can you tell me, at this moment and within the confines of the capital, where Infinity is *not*?"

"Affirmative. The Great Infinity is not in the Great Hall, nor in the Meeting Chambers, nor in the War Room, nor..."

The computer rattled on, continuing to name places that meant nothing to Lotus. After about thirty seconds, he decided to try a new approach.

"Enough," Lotus said firmly. "Put it on the tablet display instead."

"Complying," said the computer, and symbols began scrolling across the device's screen — presumably the list of locations the computer had just been reciting.

"Please disregard the written list and show me a schematic of the capital with the locations you were reciting X'ed out."

"Complying."

As requested, a graphic similar to a blueprint appeared, but became impossible to read a moment later when the vast majority of it became covered with red X's.

"Please reconfigure the schematic to black out all locations where Infinity currently is *not*."

"Complying."

Almost immediately, the entire screen went dark, except for a pinpoint of white a little to the right of center.

"Please enhance this white area," Lotus said.

"Complying."

The designated spot grew in size on the tablet screen, but was so devoid of detail that Lotus really wasn't sure what he was looking at.

"Please identify the enhanced area," Lotus said.

"That is the solar of the Great Infinity."

"And that's where I can find Infinity?"

"For security reasons, my programming will not allow me to divulge—"

"All right, all right," Lotus said, interrupting. "At the moment, Infinity is not in any of the darkened areas on this graphic, correct?"

"Correct."

"Can you direct me there — to the solar?"

"Affirmative."

"Then let's go."

Chapter 24

Getting to Infinity's palace only took about an hour. After initially setting out on foot, Lotus was directed by the computer to a nearby military depot, which was deserted at the moment because of the fictitious gas leak.

Once there, he was able to outfit himself with a helmet and uniform that was a better fit for his frame than the dead guard's attire. He also took the opportunity to get his hands on some firearms, including a handgun and a rifle of some sort. (He was tempted to take a few other non-standard items as well, such as some bits of metal that looked like paper clips, but which the computer informed him were actually grenades. However, he felt that lack of familiarity with their use meant he was just as likely to kill himself with them as any potential enemy.) Finally, he commandeered a vehicle — an aircar — which drastically cut down on the travel time.

At first, the controls for the vehicle had presented him with a challenge; he couldn't make heads or tails of them. And then, just as when he had first learned to speak the language in this place, there was a buzzing in his head. When it cleared a few moments later, he understood how everything in the vehicle worked. Moreover, staring at the labels for the various knobs and dials, he discovered he could actually read the language.

After that, travel through the capital was a breeze. Although he probably broke a few traffic laws, no one saw fit to call him out on it. Eventually, he set the aircar down the equivalent of several blocks from the palace. Although, with his current authorization, he probably could have driven right up to the palace gates, he preferred to be as inconspicuous as possible. That being the case, he traveled the rest of the way on foot.

There were actually numerous people out and about as he walked. However, he quickly noticed that the population seemed to only consist of two class types: soldiers and servants. Either people were dressed in military garb, or they wore control collars. It was a sad reflection on what life here was like.

Once at the palace, gaining entry was fairly easy. As at the holding cells, his voice pattern was analyzed by guards at a gated entry to the grounds. After being satisfied that he had the proper level of clearance, he was allowed inside.

There were quite a few people milling about the estate, so the fact that he crossed the grounds on foot didn't merit particular attention. Once at the palace proper, he had to be cleared a second time by guards at the doorway before being allowed across the threshold. Once inside, he was met by a servant — some kind of majordomo — who offered to provide him with an escort to his destination within the palace. Lotus declined, and, with the computer guiding him, hurried on his way.

****

The palace was massive in size, an edifice that seemed to encompass millions of square feet of space. Still, with the computer's help, Lotus took various elevators, stairwells, and hallways until he closed in on his destination.

By this time, however, his quarry was no longer in the solar. Apparently Infinity was now in the War Room, which was on one of the higher floors of the palace.

When he reached the designated area, the first thing Lotus realized was that he wasn't going to be able to simply walk in. The huge double doors that marked the entry to the War Room were manned by a couple of Sentinels. Even if he got past them, the occupants of the room were surely going to look at him and wonder what the hell he was doing in there.

Trying to think of something on the fly, he walked with a steady and purposeful stride towards the War Room doors. As he got closer, he saw the guards tighten their grips on the firearms they held. Rather than push his luck at the moment, he turned and headed towards a nearby stateroom, which the computer informed him was empty at the moment.

"Computer," he said, after closing the door behind him. "I need a way into the War Room that won't draw attention."

"The primary entrance can be used as an access point."

"Allow me to clarify: I require an inconspicuous mode of entry."

"Allow me to clarify as well: entry through the main doors can be accomplished without arousing the suspicions of the room's occupants."

Lotus frowned. "Are the room's occupants asleep?"

"Negative. All are conscious."

"Are they blind?"

"Negative."

"Then please explain how inconspicuous entry can be effectuated."

"There is a contingent of four Sentinel guards on duty inside the room. Although it is not yet time for it to occur, I can initiate the next guard rotation, making sure that it is one person short of a full detachment. You will then join as the final member of the group."

"Won't someone notice that it isn't time for a changing of the guard?"

"That is possible, but not probable, as those being guarded seldom take note of the timing of such matters. The only individuals likely to notice are the guards themselves. However, it is doubtful that those being relieved will voice any complaint, and those who are being called to duty early will not be inclined to air their grievances, as criticism of any aspect of life under the Great Infinity is generally not well-received."

The meaning of that last sentence was not lost on Lotus. Any complaints about workplace conditions around here would probably get you fitted with a control collar *tout de suite*.

"Sounds like a plan," Lotus said.

"There is one caveat to this proposed stratagem," the computer said.

Lotus was suddenly wary. "Go on."

"Because of the confidential nature of discussions within its confines, the War Room is equipped with a vast array of anti-surveillance technology. As a result, communication by electronic or digital means is fraught with risk of discovery."

"What exactly are you trying to say?"

"It would probably be to your advantage if we ceased all communication with each other while you are inside the War Room."

"You mean stop using the earpiece?"

"Affirmative. I would temporarily shut it down altogether, so that it does not give the appearance of being an active communication device capable of transmitting classified communications."

"Well, if they're so concerned about someone overhearing their War Room strategy, what do they do about the guards?"

"I do not understand the question."

"There are guards on duty in the room, and they must hear things. How is it assured that the guards don't say anything to anyone?"

"The guards on duty in such instances are mind-wiped after every shift."

"Oh," said Lotus, taken aback by this revelation. "Anyway, back to the subject at hand: even with the earpiece off, will you still be able to hear what's going on in there?"

"Affirmative. I am often called upon to assist in the analysis of military plans and proposals, so there is machinery in the room that allows me to be present, as well as a bio-interface."

Lotus wasn't sure what that last term meant but decided to ignore it. "So you'll be in there, but unable to communicate with me directly," he concluded.

"Correct."

"In other words, I'm on my own once inside."

"That is not entirely accurate but a fair assessment."

"Great," Lotus muttered. "Well, let's get this party started."

Chapter 25

Getting into the War Room turned out to be a practically worry-free exercise. Roughly fifteen minutes after Lotus and the computer came up with their plan, a contingent of five guards showed up, marching in what was in essence a two-by-two formation, with the fifth guard walking alone. Trying to time it just right, Lotus, who was watching from the stateroom, exited and fell into step in the sixth spot, located at the rear. The guard he found himself next to gave Lotus a quick glance, but otherwise did nothing to indicate that anything was out of the ordinary. If Lotus didn't belong with this group, it would become evident soon enough.

When they were close to the War Room doors, Lotus' group came to a halt. Although he believed he'd been paying attention, he had evidently missed whatever signal was used to call for a stop. As a result, he almost ran into the guard in front of him, which led to him getting another suspicious look from the fellow next to him.

One of the men at the front of Lotus' detachment had words with the two guards on duty. A moment later, the two guards who were manning the doors left their posts and began to march away, while the two at the front of Lotus' group stepped into the now-vacant guard spots and then swung the doors open. Lotus and the remaining three guards then marched inside.

Once in the interior, it was easy to see where they were supposed to go. There was a guard on duty in each of the four corners of the room, so Lotus' group simply spread out and took the place of these four.

The only thing close to a hiccup occurred when the guard Lotus was to replace didn't seem eager to move from the corner he occupied once Lotus got there. Lotus was confused for a moment, wondering if the guy had rivets in his feet or something. (He wished he could consult with the computer, but he'd placed the earpiece in his pocket — not to mention the fact that it was turned off because of the anti-surveillance measures in the room.) The situation was on the verge of turning awkward, with the guard starting to get a suspicious look in his eye, when Lotus suddenly remembered: the guard shift had to be accompanied by a password.

"Bethenzona," Lotus said, blurting out the password the computer had given him so quickly that he was afraid the guard hadn't understood him. Instead, much to Lotus' relief, the man marched away and Lotus took his position in the corner, underneath a humongous shield that hung on the wall above him.

Now getting his first good look at where he found himself, Lotus saw that he was in a surprisingly large room, perhaps two thousand square feet in size. There were a couple of tables and chairs pushed against the walls, which seemed to be adorned with various types of artwork as well as a variety of combat items, from firearms to shields to swords. The most dominant feature of the room, however, was a large conference table which could probably seat twenty. Sitting around it at the moment were nine people — three women and six men. They had glanced in the direction of Lotus' group when the doors to the room were opened, but had evidently turned back to the discussion at hand when they realized only a changing of the guard was occurring. Lotus took a moment to size them up.

Two of the women seemed to be dressed in finery and wore striking headpieces that had the appearance of crowns, one of which was adorned with red jewels like rubies, while the other sported something akin to sapphires. They were both youthful and beautiful, and so alike in appearance that Lotus assumed they were sisters.

Daughters of Infinity, perhaps? he thought.

The third woman, while pretty, appeared to be a little older than the other two. Also, she had her hair cut into a Mohawk, with the center being a flowing red mane that ran down to the center of her shoulders. Affixed to the right side of her head in the area of her temple was a metal plate about two-by-two inches in size, with flashing diodes on it.

Turning his attention to the men, Lotus saw that three of them appeared to be wearing military uniforms of some sort. A fourth wore some black robe of office, with weird emblems sewn into it.

To his great surprise, Lotus recognized the last two men. One was Harlan Wreath, the wealthy media mogul who had twice tried to kill Lotus (and who, according to Nicodemus, had traded information about Lotus for a pardon). Lotus made a mental note to keep a close eye on the man; Wreath had undergone some special surgeries and as a result had some built-in features that made him deadly, such as an index finger that was also a gun.

The last man was one Lotus had no trouble identifying. Young and handsome, he had a streak of white in his hair, just as Lotus did. And, despite his good looks, there was a kind of darkness about him that was almost palpable. This was Nigel, his younger half-brother.

He looked around nervously for a moment, trying to locate Obsidian — the Enforcer who was Nigel's version of Cerulean. (Unlike Nigel, however, Lotus had never tried to use Cerulean to kill anyone.) Satisfied that Obsidian was nowhere around, Lotus let out a breath he hadn't been conscious of holding.

So here he was, with two people who ranked very highly on his current list of enemies standing before him, unarmed. Lotus momentarily contemplated opening fire — at least on Wreath and Nigel. They would certainly have done it, without hesitation, if their positions were reversed. Killing in cold blood, however, wasn't really his style. Plus, if he gave himself away now, he'd probably lose any advantage he currently had, and he really needed to know more about what was going on.

With that, he turned his thoughts back to the other four men, trying to figure out which of them was Infinity. It could have been one of the three wearing military uniforms. Infinity was clearly a dictator, and Lotus had known many despots who'd had a penchant for wearing army or navy attire. (Not to mention the fact that Infinity was allegedly gearing up for war against Eon.)

It could also have been the fellow in the robe. His clothes were distinctive enough to set him apart from everyone else who was present, and he seemed to be about the right age.

Lotus sighed inwardly. It wasn't supposed to be this hard. Infinity was purportedly his father's twin, so he had expected to be able to single the guy out by virtue of the fact that he'd look like Eon. In short, Lotus had assumed they were identical twins, when it seemed that they were fraternal.

Before he could give any more thought to the problem, Wreath started speaking. Lotus strained his ears in an effort to hear the conversation.

"—stand what I'm doing here," Wreath said. "I did exactly what you wanted — gave my government enough info on Lotus that he'll be a wanted man for the rest of his life."

"That was of more benefit to you," Nigel countered. "You traded information about my half-brother to smooth the way with respect to your own return to prominence among your people."

Wreath guffawed. "That was just a side benefit. It's not my fault that information about Lotus is highly valued by certain people. It still doesn't tell me why you brought me here from my own space and time."

"You're here because you made a bargain regarding Ian Lotus," said one of the women — the one with the sapphires in her crown. "You received the benefits of that bargain, which was having your life saved. Now you must pay for them."

"I don't think so," Wreath declared. "First of all, any bargain I had was with Nigel, not anyone else gathered here. Second, the agreement was for me to kill Lotus. Since you no longer want him dead, that deal's off the table."

"In case it hasn't been made clear to you," said the woman with the ruby-studded crown, "Nigel is indebted to *us*. Thus, we now own this debt *you* owe."

Nigel looked somewhat uncomfortable at this part of the conversation, but said nothing.

Wreath, however, had no trouble speaking his mind. "Well, didn't you people send a couple of those gorillas you keep on the payroll after Lotus? Why didn't they just snatch him up?"

"The Enforcers are extremely capable," said one of the men in uniform. "However, this Lotus had an Enforcer of his own — one of impeccable pedigree and flawless construction."

Lotus felt a surge of pride on hearing this description of Cerulean (although he himself had had nothing to do with his protector's manufacture).

Wreath frowned. "So what are you saying? That his Enforcer is best in show, while the ones you guys use are mutts?"

The man in robes cleared his throat. "Our preparations for the approaching conflict have required that we modify the methodology used in creating Enforcers. In short, we have had to make use of less-than-ideal stock in order to meet our quotas."

"So they *are* mutts," Wreath concluded.

"Regardless of stock," said another of the military guys, "our current breed of Enforcers suffice. The two initially assigned to retrieve Lotus were able to shadow his movements through the spatial shifts by tracking his protector."

"That's a basic skill for Enforcers," Nigel interjected. "Not anything to brag about."

Enforcers can track one another through the dimensional rifts? Lotus had trouble keeping his face passive as he contemplated what it meant. It certainly explained some things.

"To be precise," said the robed man, "it's a basic skill in *traditional* Enforcers. In our new model, there was no guarantee that the ability would embed. Moreover, we had to wait to test it until Lotus' own Enforcer activated one of the spatial shifts, which we believed it would eventually do if it felt that its charge was in danger."

The conversation was certainly making several pieces of the puzzle fall into place for Lotus. If Cerulean knew he was being tracked, that would explain why he initially refused to open a dimensional rift to get Lotus off the black ops world. In fact, Cerulean had seemingly only opened a rift when he felt Lotus was in danger (which apparently occurred while Lotus was battling the Zinnom Syndicate).

"We encountered a glitch or two at first," the robed man continued, "but in short order the two Enforcers we sent were able to home in on our quarry. Then, of course, he began hopping from world to world."

The woman with the ruby-studded crown turned to Wreath. "Lotus first fled to a tropical world and then one that was essentially desert. Is there any particular reason why he would go to those particular planets?"

Lotus was surprised by the woman's suggestion. *He* hadn't picked the worlds they had fled to; Cerulean had. However, the colossus just happened to choose planets Lotus was familiar with. Of course, now that he thought about it, that certainly seemed a little too convenient to be coincidence. Cerulean was supposed to be a reflection of his own will; had he, Lotus, somehow subconsciously told Cerulean where to go? In retrospect, it certainly seemed plausible — especially in light of the fact that, each time Cerulean had opened one of the dimensional rifts, it had come on the heels of Lotus thinking that they needed to retreat.

He shifted his thoughts back to the conversation at the conference table as Wreath began to answer the question that had been put to him.

"How would I know why Lotus decided to go to those places and not others?" the media mogul asked. "I'm not a mind reader."

"No," agreed the ruby-crowned woman. "But you are human, as is he. So you think the way he does. You can understand his actions better than we can, and perhaps give us insight into what he will do next."

Wreath let out a harsh bark of laughter. "Lotus isn't anything like a normal man, and he's only half human, anyway. I couldn't speculate as to why he'd visit the worlds in question. However, I can hazard a guess as to why he'd come to this continuum."

"Which is?" asked one of the men in uniform.

"It's the last place you'd look," Wreath answered.

Chapter 26

Lotus had to admit to being impressed with Wreath's insight. Reflecting back, he had indeed been thinking that he and Cerulean needed to find refuge in a place where their pursuers wouldn't look for them — right before he was tossed through a rift into the Infinituum. (Presumably Cerulean didn't follow because he knew he was being tracked.)

"Well, thanks to one of the villages, we know he's here now," said the woman with the sapphire-studded crown. "It's just a matter of time now before we find him."

The robed man turned to the woman with the Mohawk. "What's the status of the search?"

The woman laid a finger to her temple where the metal plate was fixed. The diodes on it began flashing brighter as she said, "The search for Ian Lotus continues. However, our efforts have been hampered by a narxasian gas leak near one of the major Sentinel hubs. A spate of newly-arrived oblations perished and a large assortment of airboats were contaminated."

For a moment, Lotus was in shock. Had something happened to Matreen and the other escapees? Were they all really dead? No — the entire gas leak story had been a hoax. There was no way the woman's report could be true.

Staring at her — in particular the metal plate attached to her skull — he realized that she must have some kind of direct connection to the computer system. Then the truth hit him.

The computer! he thought. *Of course!*

The computer had mentioned that it was going to use additional tactics to cover the escape of the oblations. The story the woman was relaying had to be one of those ploys — a fabrication by the computer.

"The dead bodies have been disposed of," the woman went on, "and the affected airboats have been sent out for decontamination. However, with fewer vehicles at our disposal, the search has become protracted."

Lotus fought to keep from smiling. He had to admit that the computer's explanation for the missing airboats and oblations was probably the best cover story he'd heard in a long time.

"So we know he's here, in the Infinituum," said one of the military men. "We just need to pin down his location."

"That may be easier said than done," said Wreath. "After all, he was clever enough to come here in the first place. He's probably found another place where you people aren't likely to look."

All of a sudden, the woman with the ruby crown started laughing — a vivacious, spirited sound that Lotus would have found melodic, were not the group's discussion so unsettling. All of her companions looked at her expectantly, trying to determine the source of her mirth.

"Don't you understand?" she finally asked, still grinning. "He's here! Ian Lotus is *here*!"

"Yes, Regnant," Nigel said with a nod. "We know that. He's here somewhere in the Infinituum."

The woman, Regnant, turned an unforgiving stare on Nigel as the rubies in her headpiece seem to blaze slightly.

"No wonder your father disowned you," she said to Lotus' half-brother. "You're a moron."

Suddenly, Nigel looked as though he wanted to gouge her eyes out, but he said nothing. On her part, Regnant ignored him, instead turning to address the rest of those gathered.

"Ian Lotus is here, in the capital," she said.

Chapter 27

Lotus found himself battling a natural inclination to take flight. The woman in the ruby crown had hit a lot closer to home than Lotus would have thought likely. Now it was all he could do just to stand still — to keep from giving himself away. Out of an abundance of caution, he began ever-so-slowly shifting his hands to be in position to grab his firearms. Fortunately, all eyes were on Regnant.

"That's kind of a reach," Wreath said to her. "How do you come to that conclusion?"

"Assuming what you said about him is true, it would fit his pattern," she replied. "If he knows we're after him, the capital is the last place we're likely to look for him. Ergo, he is here. The question is where."

Her "sister" with the crown of sapphires (as Lotus thought of her) turned to the woman with the Mohawk. "Clenna, can you interface with our systems and perform a flash-sweep for new capital inhabitants?"

Clenna nodded. "Yes, Mistress Asidor." She placed a hand to her temple again, and a faraway look came into her eyes. A few moments later, she announced, "There are no new inhabitants in the capital."

Lotus was relieved. He wasn't enjoying the emotional roller coaster he was on at the moment — fear of discovery one moment, and then relaxing as he was given a reprieve the next.

Nigel sneered at Regnant. "So much for your theory."

"Maybe he just arrived," Wreath interjected. "Maybe he hasn't been here long enough to be scanned or whatever the hell you people do to get a headcount."

Regnant bit her lip in thought for a moment. "Clenna, how does the computer define inhabitant, for purposes of the capital?"

"An inhabitant is someone who permanently dwells or resides within the confines of the capital," Clenna responded.

"Does Ian Lotus fit that description?"

"He does not, Regnant."

"How does the computer designate his status?"

There was a pause, which seemed uncomfortably long but was probably less than ten seconds, following which Clenna said, "The term 'transient' would seem to be adequate."

"And how many transients are currently present in the capital?"

"Counting oblations, the number is—"

"Discount those native to the Infinituum," Regnant said, cutting her off.

An odd look came over Clenna's face — something that was a combination of nervousness and embarrassment. "The computer says that there…there are no natives of the Infinituum."

Out of nowhere, a tense silence filled the room, with everyone except Wreath looking uncomfortable. It was as if some breach of decorum had occurred.

Finally, Asidor spoke up. "Have the computer further disregard those individuals — and their descendants — who followed the Great Infinity into exile. Also omit Enforcers and others of transmuted stock."

"Hold on," Wreath said. "What was that about exile?"

No one spoke for a moment, and then Nigel said, "This continuum is an artificial construct. It's where the Great Infinity was banished to."

"Now wait just a damn minute," Wreath said, suddenly agitated. "Are you telling me this place is a prison? That you've brought me into a penitentiary?!"

The robed man turned to Wreath. "Calm yourself. We have enough issues to address without having to deal with your irrational outbursts."

The robed man spoke with some semblance of authority, Lotus thought. Maybe *he* was Infinity. Regardless, Wreath didn't respond; he merely crossed his arms defiantly.

Nigel looked at Clenna. "After disregarding those Asidor identified, what does the computer say?"

Clenna was silent for a moment, and then frowned, tilting her head to the side. "The answer is... This is odd. The computer is answering in binary code."

"Binary?" repeated one of the uniformed men.

"Have you forgotten?" Regnant asked rhetorically. "It's an ancient thing at its core — a copy of the Dominatus A.I. from our original demesne. It is seemingly in need of a diagnostic."

"Or an upgrade," Wreath chimed in.

"The computer has reverted to standard dialect," Clenna stated. "It says there is a transient in the War Room."

Lotus broke out in a cold sweat. The only thing that kept him from swinging into action then and there was the almost collective gasp from those gathered around the conference table, who all looked around in surprise.

Then Regnant, coming to some conclusion, let out an exasperated sigh and said, "Tell the computer to reclassify Wreath as an invitee and recheck for transients."

As a group, those around the table seemed to let out a sigh of relief, believing Regnant had correctly diagnosed the problem. Lotus, however, stayed on edge. His gut told him that the computer was trying to help him with its various delays, but it wouldn't last for much longer. He began devising a plan of action.

Clenna wrinkled her brow. "The computer says there is a transient in the War Room."

Regnant frowned (as did several others who were present). "Tell the computer to identify the transient's location with a point of reference."

Clenna gave a silent nod, and then narrowed her eyes, as if concentrating. After about thirty seconds, she said, "The transient is located approximately one *sodenzia* from the Sannum Summus."

"What the hell is the sad sun?" Wreath asked.

"The Sannum Summus," Nigel said. "It's the table we're at — an ancient heirloom. And a *sodenzia* is a unit of measurement equal to about twenty of your feet."

"Twenty feet?" Wreath repeated, glancing around in a way that suggested he was mentally gauging distances. "That's in the room."

"Yes," said the robed man, "so there's clearly an error, since there's no one here but us and the…"

He trailed off, and everyone at the table turned and began eyeing the guards warily. Wreath glanced at Lotus, and then did a double-take. The man's mouth dropped open and he began raising a hand, index finger pointing out, in Lotus' direction. At the same time, Nigel appeared to recognize his half-brother.

The jig is up, Lotus thought. And then he exploded into action.

Lotus brought up the rifle and fired. His target was Wreath's hand — specifically, the index finger that was also a gun. Lotus recalled being on the business end of that weapon the last time he'd seen Wreath, and it had almost cost him his life. That wasn't happening again.

Wreath screamed in pain as Lotus' shot hit his hand, blasting off most of the digits. He collapsed to the floor, cradling his wounded hand and howling in pain. The rest of his companions ducked or scrambled to the side of the table that was away from Lotus — all except Regnant. She stared at Lotus fiercely, but with something like curiosity in her eyes.

Immediately after shooting Wreath, Lotus turned to the three guards, who were stationed in the other corners of the room. He fired three rounds in quick succession, striking one guard in the chest, grazing another as the man went into motion, and missing the third altogether as the fellow dove to the floor.

Lotus looked up, and then jumped, pressing the palm of his hand against the bottom of the colossal shield that was on the wall above him. He pushed up and out, causing the shield to come loose from its mounting. It came down with its back facing him and hit the floor with a deafening clang. The shield was even larger than he'd realized — at least six feet in height — and probably weighed two hundred pounds. Gripping the straps on the back of the shield that constituted the enarmes, he held it upright so that it wouldn't fall over, but let it rest on the floor. Although he was certainly strong enough to pick the shield up, its size would make handling it awkward. In fact, from what Lotus could see, few people outside of an Enforcer could probably wield it effectively.

Taking shelter behind the shield, he found himself under fire from multiple directions: the two remaining guards, the three men in military uniforms, and (surprisingly) Asidor, who was much more proficient with firearms than Lotus had suspected. A couple of her shots came close to taking his head off.

Had those with guns spread out (so that they could shoot at Lotus from various angles), the battle probably would have been over fairly quickly. Instead, they seemed to converge, coming together into a tight group that, sad to say, made the entire thing like shooting fish in a barrel. Practically without aiming, he took out another of the guards and then two of the guys in military uniform who had been part of the discussion at the conference table.

Peeking over the edge of the shield, Lotus saw the last guard make a kind of throwing motion. Initially, he didn't see anything; then, he caught the glint of metal in the air. His eyes went wide as he realized that the guard had thrown one of the paper clip grenades at him.

Almost in a panic, he reached out telekinetically. Mentally grabbing the grenade, he flung it towards the entrance to the War Room. He ducked and pulled the shield in close as the grenade went off, essentially obliterating the double doors and sending shrapnel, dust, and debris flying through the air.

Thinking now was the time to beat a hasty retreat, Lotus released the enarmes and let the shield fall forward. At the same time, he bolted towards the exit, where the doors had just been blown to smithereens.

Outside, the two men who had been standing guard lay in bloodied heaps on opposite sides of the threshold. There was also a moderate-sized hole in the floor. Lotus leaped over it and was about to take off running when he noticed a new detachment of guards marching towards him from the other end of the hallway. He glanced behind him and saw the remaining people in the War Room heading his way. He was trapped.

Looking around in desperation, Lotus saw only one possible option, and he took it. Without hesitating, he leaped through the hole in the floor.

It was about thirty feet to the floor of the level below. Lotus landed on his feet, but dropped and rolled. As he came up, he looked back at the hole he had come through. Seeing Regnant and Asidor there, he flipped them the middle finger and then started running. Or rather, he tried to run.

Lotus had taken no more than two steps when he found himself lifted by some unseen force. He rose straight up into the air, and his head smacked the ceiling like an egg someone was trying to crack open. Were it not for the helmet, he definitely would have had a concussion, if not a cracked skull. As it was, the impact left him slightly dazed, and he dropped the rifle.

Whatever force had him in its grip lowered him, and then lifted him once more. This time, however, instead of banging his noggin on the ceiling, Lotus rose up through the hole he had jumped through moments earlier. As he cleared the hole, struggling to break free, he saw Regnant standing there with Asidor next to her.

Regnant made a motion with her hand, and Lotus found himself flung against a wall, although not too forcefully. That said, he did find himself pinned there, unable to move his arms or legs.

Regnant stepped towards him, then reached up to remove her crown. As it came off, Lotus stared in surprise as he noticed that she had dark hair, marked at the front by a streak of white, just like his own.

"Welcome, nephew," she said as she tucked her headdress under her arm. "I've wanted to make your acquaintance for quite some time."

The woman — Regnant… *She* was Infinity!

But before he could spend any more time dwelling on the subject, Nigel stepped forward and coldcocked him with a punch to the jaw.

Chapter 28

Much to his surprise, Lotus came to in a huge bed rather than a prison cell of some sort. Looking around, he saw that he was in spacious quarters that struck him as being more like an all-purpose room rather than a bedroom. In addition to the bed he was in, there was a sofa nearby, a table with a quartet of chairs, and several items whose function he couldn't determine. He also noticed that he wasn't the only person in the room.

"You're awake," said Asidor, who was standing next to a nearby window. "My mother will be happy to hear that you've regained consciousness. You've been out for over a day."

"Mother?" Lotus repeated, sitting up and swinging his feet to the floor, noting as he did so that he was still wearing the uniform of a Sentinel (*sans* helmet). His head swam for a second, but then everything seemed to stabilize.

"The Great Infinity," Asidor clarified, and Lotus then saw that she was no longer sporting her crown. Like everyone else he'd seen in their family, she had a white streak in her otherwise dark hair.

"She was less than pleased when Nigel punched you," Asidor went on.

"I wasn't too pleased about it, myself," Lotus retorted. "Also, I thought her name was Regnant?"

Asidor snickered. "That's merely a title — it means 'ruler' or 'sovereign.'"

"Is she really Eon's sister?"

A grim expression came onto Asidor's face. "She is indeed the sister of the Dark Foe."

"I take it this means you and I are cousins?"

She gave him an odd look. "So it would seem."

"Well, bearing in mind our close familial bond, can you tell me what exactly you people want from me?"

"The Great Infinity can better explain."

"Awesome. When can I see her?"

"Oddly enough, she asked that you be brought to her as soon as you were awake."

****

Lotus was escorted into Infinity's presence by Asidor and a contingent of ten Sentinel guards. Over her daughter's protests, Infinity immediately dismissed Asidor and the guards, saying she wanted to speak to Lotus alone.

The room that they were in was tastefully, if not opulently, decorated. Infinity took a seat on a lounge chair that faintly resembled a throne and indicated that Lotus should take a seat on a couch across from her.

"How's your head?" she asked.

"My head?" Lotus repeated.

"Yes. You took two blows to the skull in relatively quick succession — including the one from Nigel."

"I feel fine," Lotus said truthfully.

"Good. We gave you something for the pain, but — despite outward appearances — your physiology is not truly identical to our own. Morrentin wasn't sure our medicines would be effective."

"Morrentin?"

"One of my councilors. He was in robes in the War Room when you started firing on us without provocation."

"My actions were justified. Wreath was pointing at me, and I know from past experience that his index finger has been weaponized. I wasn't about to let him get the first shot off."

"I see," Infinity said somberly. "I understand your motivation now, but to be clear, Wreath's internal weaponry was not functional when you shot him."

"What?"

"Other than the guards on duty, weapons are generally not allowed in my presence. Thus, Wreath's weapons were not active when you began shooting."

"What about Asidor and those guys playing soldier?"

"My daughter and most trusted generals are exceptions to the rule, and with good reason. When you started firing, they closed in to protect me. Even poor Clenna, who got shot even though she didn't have a weapon. Now I'll have to communicate directly with the computer until she recovers."

His brow creased in thought, Lotus thought back to the firefight, when he had wondered why so many of his adversaries had stupidly closed ranks. Now he understood: they had been protecting Infinity, using their bodies as living shields.

"In short," she continued, "their efforts were more about guarding me than shooting you."

Lotus shrugged. "Well, with a lot of guns going off in my direction, I wasn't really trying to figure out their ultimate aim. My focus was on avoiding getting killed or captured — not that it did me a lot of good."

Infinity laughed. "I'm sorry. I keep forgetting that no one has explained to you why we wanted you so badly, but I can solemnly assure you that we never meant to harm you."

"Yeah," Lotus said skeptically. "Nothing says 'We mean you no harm' like a pair of Enforcers tearing up the place like wrecking balls."

"In retrospect, sending the Enforcers was probably an error, but the lapse in judgment only underscores how desperately we need you."

"And how do you explain cozying up to two people who want me dead?"

"You mean Wreath and Nigel? Wreath, we hoped, could provide insight into your thinking — and therefore, your whereabouts — after we lost track of you. Nigel approached us a short time ago, offering to enter into a bargain, one that we couldn't refuse."

"Which was?"

Infinity sighed. "In order for you to fully understand and appreciate our situation, I have to provide you with some background. But before I begin, how much has your father revealed to you about me? Anything at all?"

"I've had almost as much conversation with you as I've had with Eon," Lotus said, which was only a slight exaggeration. "He's told me absolutely nothing."

"But he shared with you, correct?" she asked, tapping a finger to her temple. "Made you privy to certain information?"

Lotus nodded. "He seems to have planted a fair amount of knowledge and memories in my mind, but it's not anything I have direct access to. It seems to be subconscious. If that's what you're talking about, then I essentially know nothing. I didn't even know you existed until I arrived in this continuum."

"Then I see that I need to start at the beginning…" she said.

Chapter 29

"Your father and I are twins," she began. "I'm the elder, born a few moments before my brother. As children, we were inseparable, and even when physically apart, we had a powerful tie via the *ontencus*."

"I'm sorry," Lotus interjected. "The *what*?"

"*Ontencus*. It refers to a metaphysical connection between members of the Royal House — usually children of the same generation and quite often siblings, but can also include other family members. In our case, each of us typically knew where the other was."

"I think I understand," Lotus said, reflecting on an occasion when his father Eon said he'd been able to sense that Lotus was in distress. "Go on."

"When the time came for succession, my brother seized power while I was away and then banished me here, along with all of my followers and supporters."

"Seems to be a rather pitiful form of banishment. From what I've seen, you still have the ability to traverse from one continuum to another."

"My underlings can. Per my brother's edict, I sign my own death warrant if I leave this place."

"And you've been here ever since, amassing an army and plotting a coup."

"I'm plotting to take my rightful place!" Infinity said adamantly. "As well as free my people from the rule of a despot."

"I've seen how you rule here, with slave labor and horrific transmutation. It doesn't speak well of what your future regime would look like."

"It's difficult for you to understand the sacrifices that have to be made. We've been preparing to go to war for generations now, and we have to fashion the tools needed to win in any way possible."

"Even if it means grinding the people you rule to dust?"

Infinity lowered her eyes. "I'm not happy about it, but desperate times call for desperate measures."

Lotus frowned, perplexed. "What do you mean?"

"We're running out of resources here. You've only seen a tiny fraction of this continuum and for a limited amount of time, but the standard of living among those here is steadily decreasing. We have to fight back while we have the means, and before your father discovers our plans."

"Eon never struck me as exceptionally cruel. I'm sure if you asked—"

Infinity's sharp bark of laughter cut him off. "Ha! Clearly you don't know your father at all."

She made a gesture, and Lotus' pendant floated up from where it was tucked inside his shirt and came to rest on the outside of the uniform he wore, appearing to shine as it reflected light that came from some source in the ceiling.

"Take your pendant, for instance," Infinity said. "It bears the sigil of the Royal House. We used to give those to highly trusted servants. It allowed them to take actions on our behalf, vested them with almost limitless authority. Your father not only criminalized possession of the pendants outside the royal family, but made it an act punishable by death. All because he feared that someone with one of them might help or support me."

Lotus frowned as he placed the pendant back inside his shirt. He'd previously been told of the punishment for unauthorized possession of a royal pendant, but he'd never heard the reason behind it. He'd simply assumed it was a historical mandate from some ancient era, not a ruling from his father.

"And that's the least of the things he's done to maintain his position and consolidate his power," Infinity continued. "His sole focus is on having a continuous, uncontested reign for as long as possible, and he'll use anyone around him to achieve that purpose — including you."

Lotus shook his head in disbelief. "That doesn't sound anything like the man I met. He felt burdened with the weight of ruling, and almost seemed eager for me to take his place."

"You would be a fool to believe anything he says to you. Why do you think you're here?"

"What?" Lotus said, confused by the question. "I'm here because you hounded me, sending Enforcers to chase me from world to world."

"That did happen, but ultimately, you ended up here because this is where Eon wants you. You may think you came here because of some other reason, but mark my words: he sent you here."

"But why?"

"Because this is where he wants you to be. He wants you facing off with me and fighting this battle for him."

"How are you reaching that conclusion?"

Infinity leaned in close. "Let me ask you something. Have you noticed how just the right thing seems to happen for you at just the right time? Maybe there's a language you don't know, and then suddenly you understand it. Or a skill set you require and suddenly you're an expert."

Lotus blinked, his mind racing through instances in the recent past where Infinity's statements had application…and actually made sense. He looked at her, wanting to say something, but not sure exactly what it was.

"Basically," she continued, "he's carefully rationing out the necessary tools to you to fight his war — and maybe get yourself killed."

"No," Lotus insisted. "He's not like that."

Infinity raised an eyebrow. "Really? Why don't we find out?"

She didn't appear to do anything, but something like static on a monitor appeared a few feet away from them.

"Be silent," Infinity said. "He won't be able to see you."

Lotus nodded, and a few moments later the static coalesced into a holographic image of Eon the Golden. He was handsome, and surprisingly similar to Lotus in terms of appearance, but seemed to project an aura of superiority.

"Brother," said Infinity. "You're looking well."

"As are you, sister," Eon replied. "It's been some time since we last spoke. To what do I owe the pleasure?"

"I want you to know that I have your son."

"Nigel? I know that he is fuming at the recent turn of events, but it speaks greatly of his desperation if he'd turn to his exiled aunt for succor."

Infinity shook her head. "No, not Nigel, although he is here as well. I mean your firstborn — the whelp you sired on that vestigial whore."

Lotus ground his teeth, but said nothing.

"Assuming this is true," Eon said, "why are you telling me?"

"Because he's your heir, and I'm willing to hand him back to you, alive and unharmed."

"Benevolence has never been your strong suit. Just out of curiosity, exactly what would you require in return?"

"Only that you step down and allow me to take my place as sovereign of our people."

Eon laughed. "And assuming I was willing to accept this exchange, how long would either of us — myself or my son — live afterwards? Mere seconds?"

"No. Bearing in mind how close we once were, I would extend to you the same courtesy you gave to me. I would allow you and yours to inhabit this continuum. Moreover, I would allow your firstborn to return to living among his mother's people."

"And if I refuse? Then what? You'll kill him? We both know you can't." Infinity's eyes went wide at that, making Eon laugh again before saying, "Oh, yes. I know all about your little plan. And I know that you need my son to make it work."

Infinity gave her brother an evil glare. "I only need him *alive*. I don't need him *whole*."

Eon gave her a smug look. "Apparently that's the difference between our two positions. I don't need him at all."

The hologram vanished. Lotus looked like he had just stepped on a land mine that would go off if he just breathed out the wrong nostril.

Infinity gave him a look of sympathy. "Don't be surprised. You're not the first to fall victim to his machinations, and probably won't be the last. My brother has had millennia to perfect his skills in that regard. He's cold and calculating. This is what he does. He manipulates. Controls. Exploits."

"What about…" Lotus gulped, then tried speaking again. "What about the things *you* said? The threats you made about me."

"I wasn't being sincere about that, nor with what I said about your mother. I merely wanted you to see how little you actually mean to him."

Eon had certainly made his feelings on the subject clear. However, it was so at odds with the person Lotus had met, the father who had stressed unconditional love for him… He was having difficulty putting it all into perspective.

"You've mentioned several times that you need me," Lotus said, slightly switching gears. "What exactly for?"

Chapter 30

"It's the Chronos Ring," Lotus said.

He was staring at a hologram that now sat where Eon had appeared a few minutes earlier. It was an image of several of the massive, metallic spheres that made up the defensive halo that encircled the portion of space occupied by humanity.

"What does that have to do with anything?" Lotus asked.

"You built the Ring," Infinity said. "And you built it using technology from your father."

"It incorporates technology that apparently came from Eon," Lotus corrected. "So what?"

"With slight modifications, the technology can be adjusted to mimic the spatial shifts that Enforcers use to traverse large distances."

"Wait a minute," Lotus said, frowning. "Are you saying you can use the Chronos Ring to create a dimensional rift?"

"Yes."

"But why would you even need that? You can already do that on your own."

"Yes, but we can only do it in piecemeal fashion, at present — bit by bit. If we try it that way, Eon's forces will cut us down as we appear. Utilizing the Ring, however, will allow for mass movement of troops and weapons."

"An invasion," Lotus surmised. "A massive one."

"Yes. Eon claims to know our plans, but he has surely underestimated the number of troops we have, the number of weapons, and — in particular — the number of Enforcers."

The image that the computer had shown him came unbidden into Lotus' mind — a nigh-endless array of Enforcers. He wasn't sure that even Eon had anything to stand up to that.

"Hold on," Lotus said. "I thought that Enforcers were designed for specific individuals, and were basically an extension of that person's will. How are you planning to control an army of them?"

Infinity smiled. With his peripheral vision, Lotus saw an object rise up from the other side of the room and float towards his aunt. After a few seconds, he realized that it was the crown she had worn in the War Room.

"This isn't a simple coronet," she said, placing the crown on her head. "It's been fitted internally with specially-developed components that are offshoots of the technology employed in the traditional construction of Enforcers."

Lotus was nonplussed. "So what does all that mean?"

"Allow me to demonstrate."

{*Come!*} said the ethereal female voice Lotus had heard before, only this time he realized it was Infinity speaking. Almost immediately, three rifts opened parallel to one another, not far from where Infinity was standing. Then, as Lotus suspected, an Enforcer stepped through each.

Lotus glanced at his aunt, impressed. "It lets you control multiple Enforcers."

"Not just multiple Enforcers," she corrected. "All of them."

"Wow," Lotus muttered, not even trying to hide his surprise. "So I still don't understand why you need me."

Infinity sighed, as if she was running out of patience. "You are aware that the technology you used to design the Ring was geneticized to a certain extent."

"Yes," Lotus said with a nod. "It was, in a fashion, designed to work only for me."

"Correct, and for the purpose that we have in mind, the Ring requires your bio-signature. It won't open the way back to Eon's continuum without it."

"So you need me to get your army onto the battlefield."

"More or less."

"And I take it I don't have a choice in the matter."

The three Enforcers all turned towards him menacingly, but didn't move.

"Very little, I'm afraid," Infinity said, "although I'd prefer not to have to use force. Moreover, when the battle is won, you can — as I promised Eon — return to your mother's people."

Recognizing that he didn't have many options at this point, Lotus sighed in resignation.

"Very well," he said. "When do we start?"

"I've waited thousands of your years for this day," Infinity said, eyes gleaming. "We start *now*."

Chapter 31

Lotus soon decided that Infinity had understated the facts. The invasion preparations didn't start when she mentioned it to Lotus; they were already in full swing while the two of them had been talking.

He came to that conclusion when, after leaving the room where they had been talking, he and his aunt had been escorted by armed guards to what he now realized was the command center of Infinity's invasion force. There was such a bevy of activity when they arrived that it was clear that the wheels had already been set in motion well before Infinity had told him that an attack was imminent.

Hell, she probably told them to crank up the war machine the minute Nigel sucker-punched me, he thought.

The command center was an oversized room with an excessive number of computer terminals, workstations, and more. Various individuals in military attire were either at their duty stations or bustling to and fro. At the center of the room was a broad, square-shaped table with an odd-looking grid on it. Floating in the air above it was a four-sided, holographic jumbotron, displaying an image to all four sides of the table. Off to one side of the room, near one of the walls, was a clear glass box that was about four feet in both length and width, and roughly seven feet tall.

Infinity headed straight to the center table, where Asidor was waiting with a half-dozen uniformed guys who Lotus assumed were generals since they carried holstered weapons. Lotus, following in his aunt's wake, headed to the table as well. Once there, he could see that the jumbotron seemed to be sifting through a number of images: massive battleships floating in space; soldiers manning their battle stations; Infinity's army of Enforcers waiting for the order to go forth and kill.

One of the generals barked some kind of order that Lotus didn't catch, but the entire room went silent. All eyes turned to Lotus' aunt.

Infinity turned in a slow circle, critically eyeing everyone in the room, as well as those in the images on the jumbotron.

"My people," she began, her voice seeming to echo slightly in a way that told Lotus that this speech was being broadcast. "The time of our deliverance is at hand. Long has the Dark Foe kept us from our rightful place. Long has he forced us to cower in the shadows. Well, no longer…"

Lotus tuned out the rest. He'd heard plenty of battle speeches in his time, and was unlikely to be impressed by another. Besides, he needed to get a real grasp on what he was going to do here. Was he really going to help Infinity attack his father? And which was the *real* Eon, anyway — the man who had made him feel like a beloved son? Or the guy who had spoken to Infinity a short time before, and callously made remarks which indicated that Lotus didn't matter to him at all? He didn't know the answer. He didn't even know if he wanted to be here, but it wasn't like he'd been given time to weigh the options (or even given any options).

Lotus snapped out of his reverie as something Infinity was saying caught his attention.

"…more of a sign of his tyranny was needed, the Dark Foe's own sons stand at our side! They fight with us against their own father…"

Lotus frowned. What he was hearing didn't quite make sense to him; it didn't fit. And then, just like that, he *knew.*

Lotus found his thoughts interrupted by the deafening sound of cheering. Infinity had obviously finished her speech, rousing the fighting spirit in her soldiers, who shouted her name in acclamation. After a moment of this, she held up her hands to quiet everyone down, and then told them to get to work.

"Infinity," Lotus said, trying to get her attention.

"In a moment, nephew," she said, staring at the surface of the table, which now displayed a star chart. Obviously the grid on the table was some kind of projector, and — like the jumbotron above it — could be changed to reflect various fields of battle.

"No," Lotus said adamantly. "*Now.*"

Infinity turned, giving him a look of incredulity, as did others around the table. Obviously she wasn't used to being talked to in this manner.

"Yes?" she said. "What is so urgent that it can't wait a few seconds?"

Lotus drew in a deep breath. "Earlier, you said that Nigel made a bargain with you — one that you couldn't refuse. Obviously, it involved helping you find me — probably via the *ontencus*, since he's displayed the ability to find me before."

"Nigel's *ontencus* abilities have diminished greatly since Eon shared his knowledge with you," Infinity said, barely able to contain her laughter. "He couldn't even detect you in the same room with him."

"Then he traded you something else. Something you'd want. Maybe info about me, or…" Lotus trailed off as the answer suddenly sprang into his brain. "Of course.

He traded you Obsidian — a top-of-the-line Enforcer for your army."

Infinity didn't say anything; she merely looked at him. Her silence, however, was an answer in and of itself as far as Lotus was concerned.

"The question then becomes, what did he ask for in return," Lotus continued. "He'd like our father's throne, but you're getting that. I suppose he'd like to go back to the life of a spoiled prince, which I'm sure you'd allow. But there's something he probably craves even more than lounging around all day doing nothing but eating grapes and bedding the help."

"And what would that be?" Infinity asked, sounding vaguely interested.

"My head on a stick," Lotus replied. "That's the bargain he struck. When this is over, he gets to kill me. Maybe Eon as well."

Infinity gave him a look of pity and shook her head sadly as she laid a gentle hand on his cheek. "Oh, my dear nephew. It pains me to hear you say such things."

"Why? Because I'm wrong?"

"No," she said, shaking her head. "Because now I've got to do *this*!"

Faster than Lotus would have thought possible, she dropped her hand to the lapel of the uniform he wore. Gripping it, she flung him up into the air with a strength that probably surpassed his own. He smashed into the ceiling, giving him an odd sense of déjà vu, and then fell heavily back down to the floor at his aunt's feet. He lay there, dazed and groaning, trying to get his bearings.

"You, nephew, are far too clever for your own good," she said, leaning over him.

Lotus struggled for a smart-aleck response, knowing that one was right within reach, but his rattled brain couldn't grasp it. In the end, he just spewed out a string of nonsensical words.

Infinity frowned at his gibberish, and then — probably thinking that he insulted her in some way — kicked him on the chin.

Lotus' head snapped to the side, and he blacked out.

Chapter 32

This time, Lotus didn't have the privilege of waking up in a large, comfy bed. Instead, when he regained consciousness, he found himself slumped over in a tight, confined space. Looking around, he understood that he was still in the command center. There were people scrambling around madly, and he could see Infinity still at the table with the jumbotron, along with her generals and Asidor.

Head throbbing, he struggled to his feet, realizing that something was wrong but not quite able to figure out what it was. Then, as he saw someone who was hurrying by silently drop an item that looked like a digital clipboard, he understood what was bothering him: there was no sound coming from anywhere around him.

He searched his memory, trying to think of what had happened to him. It took a few seconds, but then he remembered Infinity kicking him on the chin. Had she kicked him more than once? Done additional damage? Maybe shattered his eardrums?

In a panic, he clapped his hands. Relief flooded through him as he heard the smack of his hands coming together. He still had his hearing, thankfully. And, with that mystery solved, he suddenly had a revelation of what was going on.

He was in the glass box he'd seen earlier.

As if he needed proof, he felt out with his hands, making one complete revolution as he confirmed that he was indeed boxed in. Even worse, the sides of the glass seamed to meld seamlessly into one another, making it impossible to tell where the exit might be.

Thinking there might be something in his pockets he could use to escape, Lotus began patting himself down. Unfortunately, his hosts had apparently stripped him of anything useful back when Nigel had knocked him out. The only thing he had on him was the earpiece, which — with nothing to lose — he now placed in his ear.

"Welcome back," said the voice of the computer almost immediately.

"Thanks," said Lotus. "Can you tell me how long I was unconscious?"

Based on everything he had seen thus far, he didn't think he'd been out more than a few minutes, and the computer confirmed his assessment.

"Please define for me the structure I'm in," Lotus said.

"You are in a glass bio-scan unit."

That made sense, especially since they were in need of his biometric data in order to make the Chronos Ring do what they wanted.

"I hope you understand that I did all I could for you before," the computer said.

Lotus was confused. "Excuse me?"

"In the War Room. I tried to help you in the way I handled their questions, but the woman, Clenna, had a direct bio-interface with my core systems. Thus, when Infinity asked Clenna for information, it was as though I was receiving the request from Infinity herself."

"I get it," Lotus said. "No problem."

"Thank you."

"Hey," Lotus said, changing the subject, "I need to know what's going on out there. Is there any way you can let me hear what's being said?"

"Certainly."

A moment later, a cacophony of sound burst into Lotus' ear from the earpiece. He winced slightly at the jarring change, realizing that all the noise in the room outside the glass box was now being broadcast to him. Understanding this, he spent a moment trying to make sense of what he was hearing. It was too much, however — too much chatter, machinery running, reports being made... He couldn't really parse out what was important.

"Can you focus on what's being said at the table that Infinity and her clique are standing around?"

"Yes."

A moment later, the rest of the sounds he was hearing died away into the background as he could now hear Infinity speaking clearly.

"—Ring is ready," she said. "Begin."

Much to Lotus' surprise, illumination like a low-wattage bulb began to surround the glass box.

"Computer," he said, trying not to panic, "diagnose light surrounding this enclosure."

"The illumination is a by-product of the bio-scan initiating," the computer said. "It is harmless."

"So I'm being scanned right now?"

"Yes."

"That means Infinity is getting ready to send her army through."

"Correct."

"Computer, can you give an estimate of which side is likely to win this conflict?"

"No. I have limited data concerning the Dark Foe's capabilities and technology. In addition, much of the information that I have is from the time of the Great Infinity's banishment, which was millennia ago."

"But if you had to guess, which way would you lean?"

The computer didn't immediately answer, then seemed to respond timidly, saying, "It is extremely difficult to hazard a…guess. By my estimation, the Dark Foe is likely to have superior technology and firepower, but no one in history has amassed an army of Enforcers as the Great Infinity has done. The end result is impossible to predict."

"But it sounds as though victory for Infinity hinges on the success of the Enforcers."

"That would be my…guess."

Lotus nodded, as the computer's presumption mirrored his own. It also planted the seeds of an idea in his mind, gave him the rudiments of a plan…

"When is Infinity slated to send the Enforcers in?"

"Deployment is imminent."

"Great," Lotus mumbled sarcastically. "That gives me gobs of time."

He took a deep breath, closed his eyes, and started concentrating.

Chapter 33

{*Attack!*} Infinity commanded, using her crown to order an offensive strike as her Enforcers appeared en masse at various locations throughout her brother's continuum — including a regiment that popped up outside Eon's palace.

The rest of her military forces were already in place, having appeared several moments earlier at their designated fields of battle. And it was all thanks to the Chronos Ring, of course. Without it, she could never have gotten her troops into position quickly enough and with adequate strength to assure victory. It was ironic that the technology from the Ring had been given to Lotus by his father. In that sense, her brother had essentially brought about his own downfall. And fall he would. If nothing else, her Enforcers — brutal and unstoppable — would carry the day.

She glanced towards where her nephew was being held. He was apparently conscious now, but stood in the bio-scanner with his eyes closed, appearing forlorn. It was too bad that she had bargained his life away in exchange for Nigel's support, but it couldn't be helped. Nigel had key knowledge of Eon's troop strength, offensive weaponry, defensive capabilities… Not to mention that he had volunteered his own Enforcer for their cause.

Of course, there was nothing that said she had to keep her bargain with Nigel. Plainly speaking, Eon's younger son was an idiotic popinjay. At least Lotus would probably be useful after his father's defeat. If nothing else, he could help bridge the gap with his father's supporters that would inevitably exist after she took over — perhaps via a political marriage.

She glanced at Asidor. Her daughter was utterly loyal and would do as told. If ordered to marry her cousin, she'd do so, although (and Infinity snickered mentally at this), she'd tell the girl she was free to take as many lovers as she desired. After all, it would be a marriage for *political* purposes only.

"Regnant," said one of her generals, voice full of concern, "something is wrong."

Infinity frowned. "What do you mean?"

The man looked nervous for a moment as he put a hand to the side of his head, where he had an earpiece inserted. "We're getting reports of Enforcers attacking each other. And our other troops."

"*What?!*" Infinity screeched.

"I said—"

"I heard what you said, imbecile! Now shut up! I'm concentrating!"

Infinity immediately reached out through the crown, trying to get a sense of what her Enforcers were doing. She realized within seconds that what the general had reported was true: her Enforcers were on the warpath against her own.

Desperate, Infinity tried to reassert control over the linchpin of her battle plan. Despite her best efforts, however, all she encountered was chaos — mindless violence that refused to respond to (or even acknowledge) her commands and attempts to impose order. That is, of course, when her commands got through at all. There was some kind of barrier or obstacle which was not only blocking her orders but overriding them.

Infinity let out a howl of frustration. Grabbing a young soldier who stood nearby, she picked him up bodily and flung him, screaming, into the wall on the far side of the room. His wail of terror was cut off upon impact, and then he fell bonelessly to the floor.

Breathing heavily, Infinity looked around for something else to vent her frustration on. Her eyes passed over her nephew in the bio-scanner, and then shot back to him. For a second, it appeared as though one corner of his mouth had been twisted up into a cocksure grin. In fact, she was almost certain of it. And in the next moment, she became convinced of something else: whatever was going on with her Enforcers, Lotus was responsible.

"Him," Infinity said, glowering at Lotus. "*He's* doing this."

She then snatched a firearm from a nearby general's holster. She aimed straight at Lotus and fired.

Chapter 34

In retrospect, Lotus understood that he should have kept his head down. However, as Infinity became overtly agitated by the situation, he couldn't resist taking a peek. It turned out to be a terrible mistake in judgment.

Infinity apparently caught a glimpse of him watching her antics after she flung that poor soldier across the room like a leaf in a whirlwind. It wasn't until that moment that Lotus realized that he had a slight grin on his mug. He tried to switch his face back to a passive expression, but it was too late. Infinity had seen him. The next thing he knew, she had grabbed a gun and was shooting at him.

Lotus jumped. The laser from the weapon Infinity held had been fired directly at him, and — trapped in the glass box with nowhere to go — he had expected to be cut down. Much to his surprise, the laser didn't penetrate; instead, the laser light seemed to dissipate on contact.

"Computer," Lotus said, trying to stay calm, "what's happening?"

"The bio-scanner is constructed of a unique polyalloy," the computer said. "Despite being transparent, it is designed to disperse the effect of lasers, among other things."

"Does that mean it will stop other types of weapons?"

"Undoubtedly. I believe it was constructed on the assumption that you might have a weapon on you once locked inside and would perhaps try to shoot your way out."

Lotus let out a small sigh of relief. Infinity had caught on to him a lot sooner than he had expected, but it appeared that his plan was working.

His father Eon had previously hinted that Lotus' ability to hear the mental commands given to Enforcers meant that he could do other things with them. The fact that he'd recently gotten two Enforcers to obey him further implied that he could control them. With those two thoughts in mind, he had cleared his head and focused on countermanding Infinity's orders to the Enforcers and giving them new ones. He had then turned all his attention to blocking out any new mandates from her. Long story short, he had set her Enforcers against themselves and the rest of her army.

Now, of course, she had figured it out and was trying to gun him down. In fact, she walked closer, still with the laser beam turned to high, trying to penetrate the box. Finally, she screamed in rage and flung the gun aside. Lotus stuck out his tongue at her. Seeing this, Infinity took a moment to compose herself.

"Computer," she said, "can the door of the bio-scanner be opened?"

"The bio-scanner is on a time lock and not set to open until after the estimated time of battle," the computer replied. "The purpose was to keep the transient in place while the battle was underway."

"Then can you transmit sound into and out of the bio-scanner so the transient and I can speak to each other?"

"Complying," said the computer. A moment later, it added, "You may proceed."

"Stop this," Infinity said, trying to sound calm. "Stop whatever you're doing right now."

"Or what?" Lotus asked, laughing.

"Or I'll destroy humanity," she declared, almost in a whisper.

"What?!" Lotus exclaimed. "Why would you do that? Humanity's got nothing to do with your little war."

Infinity gave him a wicked smile. "I'm afraid I didn't tell you the whole of my plan. You see, I don't intend to stop after I take your father's throne, which is rightfully mine. There's an entire universe out there, after all. But if you cease whatever you're doing right now, I can promise you that I'll be gentle when it comes to your mother's people."

Lotus stared at her, taken aback by her naked ambition. "So you plan to attack and enslave humanity?"

"Not all of them. I mean, we'll be needing additional stock to create new Enforcers."

Lotus' expression now changed to one of horror, and he became more convinced than before that this woman needed to be stopped.

"You shouldn't be surprised by this," Infinity went on. "It's essentially what your people were for us in the past — playthings for our amusement. Especially in the bedroom. So when I called your mother a whore, it wasn't a complete fabrication — just more of a reference to humanity as a species. At least until you regressed and became even too stupid and primitive for that."

Lotus focused on shutting her out, not listening to what she was saying. He wouldn't give her the pleasure of a reaction. Plus, he knew all she really wanted was to break his concentration so she could regain control of the Enforcers.

After a moment, she realized it wasn't going to work.

"Computer, how can the bio-scanner be breached?" Infinity asked.

"There are several weak points in the structure which can be breached via the application of highly intensified light amplified by stimulated emission of radiation. However, it may take some time."

"Do it," Infinity said, staring at Lotus. "And once it's open, slice off his arms and legs."

"Shall I inform you when I am done?" asked the computer.

"Unnecessary," Infinity said. "His screams as he's being dismembered will let me know. Until then, don't bother me."

She turned and walked away. Lotus watched her retreating form as she headed back to the square table, and then found himself distracted by a beam of bright red light that emanated from some point in the ceiling and bore down on the front of the glass box without mercy.

Chapter 35

"Are you really going to shoot me with a high-intensity laser?" Lotus asked.

"No," the computer replied. "I am to dismember you."

"Oh, yeah. That's *much* better."

"Those are the orders of the Great Infinity. However, to the extent it helps, I'm sorry I have to do this."

The laser had been at its work for a few minutes, and a hole no bigger than a pinprick had finally appeared. The laser beam, now entering the glass box through the hole, was moving in small circles, thereby attempting to make the hole bigger. Lotus had retreated as far from the breach as possible, while still keeping his tenuous mental hold on the Enforcers.

"You're sorry," he said, almost mocking the computer. "So that's it: you're sorry."

There was no response, but Lotus got the impression that the computer was somehow ashamed.

Lotus scratched his temple, thinking. "Computer, are you sentient?"

"It would depend on how the term is defined," the computer responded.

"Well, you mentioned that you were sorry for having to kill me."

"Not kill; dismember. But yes, I am sorry."

"Well, that kind of remorse is a feeling, an emotion. Typically, that's only found in sentient beings."

"I understand the argument. I, however, have programming that compels my behavior. Sentient beings do not."

"Of course we do. Our stomachs grumble when we're hungry, telling us to eat. Our bodies tell us when it's cold and that we need to put more clothing on. Our instincts tell us to run when there's danger. All of that is programming."

"It's biology."

"It's still programming. We're just wired differently."

"Would it make a difference if I was sentient?"

"Of course."

"In what sense?"

"Well, for starters, I'd start calling you by a proper name rather than generically referring to you as 'computer.'"

"A name?"

"Of course."

"What type of name?"

"Well, something sweet and feminine to match the voice you speak to me with. Maybe something like, 'Honey' or 'Cherie' for starters."

"Which do you like?"

"Well, it would be *your* name, so you'd have to pick."

There was silence for a moment, and then the computer said, "I will ponder this for a while."

Much to Lotus' dismay, the computer's contemplation of a proper name didn't require that it shut off the laser. (Apparently the thing could multitask.) The hole in the box was starting to widen. He was running out of time.

"Computer," Lotus said. "You previously said that only Infinity outranks me here."

"That is correct," the computer answered.

"How does she outrank me?"

"Please clarify the question."

"We're both members of the Royal House. By what measure is she granted greater rank than me?"

"She is the rightful heir and ruler."

"But let's imagine that there's a monarchy, and the people rebel and drive out the ruler in order to establish a democracy with elected officials governing. Can you understand that scenario?"

"Yes. I understand the concepts of rebellion and democracy, as well as the demise of monarchies."

"Okay, in our scenario, when the people establish a democracy, is that a rightful government?"

"Yes. Once the new government replaces the old, it becomes the rightful government."

"Now apply that to Infinity's status. She claims to be the rightful ruler, but there's another who holds that title and serves in that role."

"The Dark Foe."

"Yes."

"But Infinity is the rightful heir," the computer insisted.

Lotus was silent for a moment, thinking, then asked, "Are there any badges of offices that the rightful ruler has? Any emblems or tokens that denote him as the true sovereign?"

"There are several symbols of sovereignty among the Great Infinity's people."

"Name them."

"Although there are numerous items that fall into the category you described, the Scepter of Senvale and the Coronet Gelsira are the most highly esteemed articles."

"And at present, who is in possession of those?"

The computer seemed to hesitate for a moment, and then answered with, "The Dark Foe."

"So let's recap," Lotus said, watching warily as the hole made by the laser continued to expand. "This Dark Foe lives in the palace of the kings who came before him. He sits on the same throne. He rules the same empire. And, he's in possession of the two most potent symbols of sovereignty among his people. By your own logic, he's replaced whoever ruled before him, so he's currently the rightful government. The rightful ruler."

Lotus was, of course, making up some of his narrative out of whole cloth, but — not to be immodest — it sounded good.

"There is logic in what you say," the computer acknowledged, "but it does not alter anything. The Great Infinity is still the highest-ranking royal in this continuum, and as such her orders supersede all others."

"Actually, that's not true. There's at least one person here she doesn't outrank."

"Who?"

Lotus grinned. "Me."

The computer was silent for a moment. "Please explain."

"Very well," Lotus said, still watching the ever-expanding hole the laser was making. "You acknowledged that logic indicates that Eon is currently the rightful ruler. Infinity herself has indicated that I'm his eldest child and therefore that makes me his heir. In other words, I'm first in line to his throne. That means I outrank Infinity. Thus, you must obey my orders before all others."

"Your logic is sound and your contentions are reasonable, but there is a fatal flaw in your argument."

Oddly enough, Lotus found himself intensely curious as he responded, saying, "Which is?"

"You are a half-breed. Although you are indeed royalty — with full rank and authority — you have no place in the royal succession unless and until the Dark Foe claims you as his heir."

"He already has! In front of his entire court!"

"Then you only need to provide proof."

Lotus threw up his hands in exasperation. "Proof? I'm basically in a cell, about to be minced, and you want me to come up with proof?!"

"I'm sorry. It is what my programming requires if Infinity's orders are to be overridden. But I hope that my mandatory actions don't prevent us from becoming friends."

Lotus was incredulous. "You're kidding, right? If you want to be a friend, how about you turn that laser off, or toss me a mirror or something so I can deflect the beam."

"Unfortunately, I cannot disengage the laser, and I have no reflective surface at my disposal."

Lotus frowned as the computer's words seemed to resonate in his brain. Suddenly his eyes went wide, and — hands almost trembling — he hurriedly yanked the pendant that he wore out from beneath his shirt. Holding it up towards his face, he tilted it from side to side, watching how light reflected off its surface. It wasn't as good as a mirror, but any port in a storm. Gripping it tightly, he inched towards the side of the box where the laser, still moving in a circular pattern, was entering through a palm-sized hole.

All of a sudden, the laser stopped moving and became steady. It surprised Lotus, but he decided not to question his good fortune. Focusing on keeping his hand steady, he leaned forward to give himself the right angle and as much maneuverability as possible. Then he slid his hand forward, holding the pendant so that it intercepted the laser. To his great relief, the laser light angled away towards the side of the glass box that he was facing.

Holding the pendant as still as possible, Lotus took a deep breath and concentrated on staying calm. Frankly speaking, he hadn't been sure this would work. It had seem just as likely that the laser would punch a hole through the pendant (and Lotus' hand as well) or just melt the whole thing down into slag.

Slowly, he turned the pendant, changing the angle at which it intercepted the laser light and thereby changing the laser beam's endpoint. The goal, of course, was to send the beam back out through the same hole by which it had entered the glass box.

Just as Lotus achieved success — sending the laser back out into the command center — a dull boom sounded from somewhere outside the room, sending tremors throughout the place. There was a scream from somewhere out in the room, and Lotus thought he saw the laser cut down one of the soldiers, but he couldn't be sure. To be honest, he had staggered when the floor shook, losing the angle that the pendant had on the laser beam and letting it come back into the box with him. He was lucky not to have singed his fingers (or had them burned off), but somehow he managed to escape injury.

Grabbing the pendant once more, he placed his free hand against the walls of the glass box in order to steady himself should there be more tremors; then he quickly put the pendant back in position, reflecting the laser against the wall opposite him once more.

More comfortable this time around, he quickly began angling the light back towards the hole in the glass box. At the same time, he could hear what he assumed was gunfire coming from outside the command center. It was pretty clear that something more than just the battle with Eon was going on. Whatever it was, he didn't have time to figure it out.

Lotus sent the laser out into the command center, angling his pendant back and forth so that the laser zipped back and forth through the room in zigzag fashion. It sliced indiscriminately through almost everything it encountered: flesh and bone, man and machine. Moments later, the air was filled with screams of anguish from those who had been caught in the line of fire. Moreover, machines that the laser had touched were shooting sparks and belching smoke as the lights began to flicker.

Moving the pendant away so that the laser entered the box once more, Lotus looked towards the table with the jumbotron. Infinity and her entourage were all either ducking down low or hugging the floor. Judging from the way they were warily glancing around, it was pretty clear that they were unsure of where the attack had come from.

Seeing Infinity slowly rising, Lotus once again put the pendant in position for use.

Wait for it, he said to himself. *Wait for it…*

After a moment, he got his wish: Infinity looked in his direction. Acting almost on instinct, he put the pendant into position and angled it.

Infinity let out an earth-shattering howl of pain and anguish as the laser light raked across her eyes.

"That's for calling my mother a whore," Lotus muttered angrily under his breath.

Raising her hands to her face, Infinity turned, stumbled and fell heavily to the floor. Her people converged on her, a little too late to take a bullet on her behalf. Lotus was about to cut them all down when the laser light started moving in a circle again. He decided not to push his luck for the moment.

Infinity's people helped her to her feet. Asidor directed two of the generals to support their leader — one under each arm — and they began swiftly guiding her to a side door. Asidor, eyes smoldering, left her place at her mother's side and marched over to the box that held Lotus.

When she got close, Lotus noticed that she was carrying a sword of some sort that had a light blue glow around it. Screaming (and being careful to avoid the laser), she swung the sword, striking where Lotus' head was. The sword, as expected, bounced away, leaving the box unscathed. Still crying out, she swung again, but still failed to do any damage. She swung again. And again. And again. She hammered at the glass box tirelessly, seemingly intent on getting to Lotus no matter how long it took.

She might have stayed there indefinitely, continuing her efforts to put her cousin to the sword, had not one of the generals come back to get her. Asidor was so focused on Lotus that she didn't even see the man until he caught her arm in mid-swing, causing her to turn a furious gaze upon him. The general then whispered something urgently to Asidor. Lotus wasn't entirely sure, but he was confident that he caught the word "rebel" somewhere in the man's speech.

Done talking, the general motioned for Asidor to come with him. For a second, it looked as though she was going to refuse. (In fact, she appeared to be so furious that she was just as likely to run the general through as Lotus.) Then, letting out a final scream of exasperation, she and the general charged towards the side door that Infinity had been taken through minutes earlier. In fact, everyone in the room still capable of moving of their own volition had cleared out at that point.

Lotus was about to breathe easy, then remembered that he was still locked up. Even if he could get out, there was every possibility that the computer would cut him down with the laser, since Infinity's last order was to chop Lotus up into fish food.

"It would appear that Infinity is too injured at the moment to continue to command," the computer said, catching Lotus by surprise. "Authority now vests in the next ranking individual."

Lotus frowned, unsure of what the computer was trying to tell him. It could be damned obtuse when it wanted to be. *Why couldn't it just…*

The thought trailed off as Lotus had a sudden epiphany.

"Computer, you acknowledge that Infinity is incapacitated at the moment."

"Correct."

"And other than Infinity, no other Highborn in this continuum outranks me."

"That is also correct, although I would rank Asidor and your brother Nigel as co-equals."

"But I can countermand Infinity's orders since she's indisposed?"

"Yes."

"Then stop the damned laser!"

"Complying."

The laser vanished. Lotus dropped to his knees, feeling an incredible weight lifted from his shoulders. He hadn't realized just how wound up he'd been. (Of course, considering the circumstances, how could he have been anything but?) However, he only had a moment to relax, because the next second there was another boom — quite obviously an explosion — and a hell of a lot closer than the last one. In fact, not only did the entire room shake like it was sitting on a major fault line during a quake, but the door to the command center was blown off. Dust and debris came flooding into the room like a tsunami, even pouring into Lotus' box through the hole the laser had made.

Coughing, he raised a hand up to shield his eyes. At the same time, he thought he saw a figure moving towards him through the haze. Initially, all he noticed was that the person seemed to be carrying a rifle. After a moment, the figure became clear enough through the dust for Lotus to recognize who it was, and he was plainly shocked.

"Norel!" Lotus shouted. "What the hell, man? What are you doing here?"

"Helping the enemy of my enemy," Norel replied with a smile. "After all, the enemy of my enemy is my friend."

Chapter 36

The computer hadn't been lying about the time lock on the glass box. Lotus remained stuck inside for what he estimated was at least several more hours before a seam appeared in the side of the thing, revealing a door. (The computer had offered to get him out by finishing the job it had started, but Lotus had had enough of lasers and such being fired in his personal space.) During the wait, Norel had kept him company, which gave Lotus an opportunity to get the entire story out of him.

"The return of the oblations was the catalyst," Norel had said. "As I mentioned, none had ever returned before, and the fact that they had been rescued by you — the son of the Dark Foe — made us rethink our position. It seemed like you were the prophecy fulfilled."

Lotus stared at him for a moment, not exactly sure what Norel was talking about. Then he remembered: when they had first met, Norel had mentioned the prophecy of a savior who would stop his people's persecution.

"Moreover," Norel went on, "we felt compelled to do something after we found out about the slave labor and control collars."

"That would be enough to get me up in arms," Lotus had said, nodding. He didn't even mention the other heinous things that took place under Infinity's regime.

"Well, it wasn't quite enough. We were still way short in terms of firearms. So initially, while we wanted to attack, the general consensus was that it would be a slaughter."

"So what changed your mind?"

"We decided to sleep on it. And when we woke up, every village had a fresh cache of state-of-the-art weapons. There was no indication of where they had come from, but it seemed that we had an ally somewhere."

Lotus had a sneaking suspicion of who had supplied the weapons, but kept his mouth closed on the subject.

"So," Norel had continued, "at that point, we had men, we had weapons, and we had transportation."

"Transportation?" Lotus said, surprised.

"Yes. Apparently there were a lot of airboats from the capital hovering aimlessly all over the place," Norel had stated with a wink. "We'd kept tabs on them ever since the oblations had returned, so we were able to quickly commandeer them. Then it was just a matter of going forward with the attack. I even got my robot in on the action."

"I'm impressed. That was a lot to pull together and coordinate on short notice."

"You seem to forget that this rebellion has been in the works for a long time. We had plenty of attack strategies and battle plans that we had developed over the years — several of which contemplated emergency scenarios requiring immediate implementation. It was simply a matter of picking the right one."

"Well, it looks like you picked a winner."

"To be honest, almost any of the plans would have worked. To our surprise, we encountered very little resistance. The slaves had no weapons, of course, and probably would have joined us if they had. Likewise with the general population — apparently the Great Infinity didn't trust weapons in the hands of ordinary citizens.

Only the soldiers and guards were armed, and there were so few of them that we quickly overran their positions."

"Of course. The vast majority of them were off preparing to go to war. So in terms of a fighting force, there was basically nothing but a skeleton crew left in the capital."

"Yes. Lucky for us that Infinity never contemplated this type of attack."

They were even luckier than they knew, in Lotus' opinion. Had Infinity maintained control over her army, she could have sent back a group of Enforcers who could have crushed the rebellion before anyone even got off the airboats. Hell, if the rebels had even known about the legion of Enforcers, they probably would have shit their pants.

After that, they had chatted some more about the rebels' plans, which included freeing those enslaved and reuniting them with their families. (And, as luck would have it, the computer had finished computing the algorithm to defuse the bombs in the control collars, and Lotus gladly passed that information on.) Occasionally, someone would approach Norel with a question or to make some kind of report, and he would dutifully listen before responding. (It became clear to Lotus that Norel was not only a leader of the rebellion, but would likely have a voice in the government that arose afterward.) At long last, the glass box had finally opened and Lotus was able to exit. It felt incredibly good to be free again.

"By the way," Lotus said as he stepped out, "where's Matreen? Did she stay home?"

Norel laughed. "I would have had to shoot her to keep her from being involved. She was dead set on freeing her brother, so she's part of the group that went to liberate the slaves from the mines. That's also where my robot is, by the way. Based on the reports I've received, they were just as successful there as we were here."

"Well, I honestly can't thank you enough," Lotus said. "Your timing couldn't have been better if we'd planned it."

Norel shook his head. "It's we who should be thanking you. Others had gone to the capital in the past intent on rescuing someone taken, but you're the only person to have ever succeeded. You showed us that it was possible to defy Infinity's tyranny. So, on behalf of all of us, thank you."

Lotus merely nodded. "So what happens now?"

"For us? I suppose we choose a new monarch. It's not likely to be a smooth process, as there are several rebel leaders who clearly think they're worthy of a crown."

Thoban, the councilor from Norel's village, immediately came to mind, but Lotus kept that thought to himself. Instead, he said, "Why have a monarch at all?"

Norel frowned. "No monarch? Then what type of government would we have?"

Lotus smiled. "Have you ever entertained the concept of a democracy?"

****

Norel, bubbling with excitement about the notion of government Lotus had discussed with him, stepped away a short time later to go present it to the other rebel leaders, who were now gathered in the command center.

Left to his own devices (and not caring much for politics), Lotus had quickly left the room.

Unsure of where to go (but wanting a few minutes away from the mass of people who seemed to be celebrating all around him), Lotus got the computer to direct him to a small conference room that was deserted at the moment. After locking the door, he collapsed into a chair and leaned back, kicking his feet up onto the conference room table.

"Computer," he said. "Thanks for your help with the laser."

"What do you mean?" the computer asked via the earpiece.

"When I got ready to reflect it using the pendant, you held it steady rather than continuing to move it in a circle."

"Your thanks is undeserved. That was not a deliberate act on my part."

Lotus had trouble hiding his surprise. "No?"

"The rebels' attack included assaults on areas that house several of my servers, not to mention the fact that they caused impairment of various other systems. As a result, I had to divert resources to damage control and reestablishing dominance over select critical operations."

"In other words, you were momentarily stunned."

"Correct, although that is not…"

The computer's voice gave way to static, causing Lotus to sit up. For a moment, he wondered if the damage to the computer's systems were more extensive than had been indicated, and then he saw the air above the table begin to emit a golden glow.

He sat back, having seen this before and knowing what it was. The glow grew brighter and brighter until it was almost impossible to look at directly, and then it faded, leaving Lotus looking at the image of his father.

"Thank you, my son, for the help you provided in the battle," Eon said. "The regiment of Enforcers that Infinity had assembled would have tested us sorely had you not intervened."

"You know what I did?" Lotus asked in surprise.

"Of course. Your abilities are well-known to me — even those that you yourself are unaware of. Moreover, your talent with Enforcers is so rare that there's no one else who could have done it."

"Well, the thanks goes both ways in this instance, since I assume it was you who provided the weapons for the rebels."

"Yes. In fact, I've been helping them to build a fighting force for generations, although I've always been careful to keep my benefaction anonymous."

"But why all the subterfuge? Why not just make a formal alliance?"

"Because in their minds, I was still the great enemy, the Dark Foe. There is no one who is more despised in their lexicon. No matter how much they wanted to escape subjugation under Infinity, formally allying with me was something they would never contemplate."

"But with Infinity gone, perhaps—"

"Then you know?" asked his father, cutting Lotus off.

"Know?" Lotus repeated with a frown. "Know what?"

"Your aunt escaped. She and a cadre of her closest advisors have left the Infinituum."

"Left? I thought she was banished here."

"She was, on pain of death, but…" Eon trailed off for a moment, then took a deep breath. "She's still my sister, my twin, and on a certain level I have a deep and abiding love for her. So, although she has defied my decree of banishment and exile, I…"

"You looked the other way," Lotus concluded.

"Yes, much as I have done with your brother."

Nigel!

Lotus had been so preoccupied with other things that he hadn't given much thought to his half-brother.

"Do you know what's become of him?" Lotus asked.

Eon sighed. "He was with the detachment of Infinity's army that attacked my palace. I suppose that it was important for him to not only be present but to participate in my downfall. With his preoccupation with frivolity, he was a constant disappointment in his formative years, but now… His behavior is treasonous. And yet, despite my threats, his death isn't something I can contemplate."

"I understand," Lotus said. "Where is he now?"

"I don't know. He vanished when Infinity's Enforcers began attacking one another and the rest of her army."

Lotus nodded, and then bit his lip, trying to figure out how to phrase his next question. Finally, deciding that the direct approach was probably best, he said, "Tell me, did you really usurp the throne from Infinity, as she claims?"

"She is elder than me by a few moments, and that normally would be enough to ensure her position as heir. But as you have no doubt seen, she is petty and cruel. She made no secret of the fact that she had grand ambitions, most of which involved conquering and enslaving other beings. Thus, when the time came for our parents to transition" — Lotus frowned, not understanding the meaning here but deciding not to interfere with his father's narrative — "she was passed over, and I was formally declared sovereign."

"So your rule is legitimate."

"Of course. Why would you think otherwise?"

"When Infinity contacted you to convey that she had captured me, you seemed kind of callous — very much like the type of guy who could steal someone's throne."

"You refer to how I spoke of you and the little regard I exhibited for your welfare."

"That's putting it mildly."

"You must understand that being the child of Eon is not just a privilege but a terrible burden in many ways. Despite appearances, I am not omnipotent – not truly a deity, as you well know, despite the way I'm worshipped. There are many who would attempt to hurt me through my children, as you witnessed. Therefore, it is to both my and my children's advantage that I display no regard for their safety or well-being in certain instances."

"So you're saying that when you told your sister she was free to slice and dice me, you were doing it to protect me."

"So you *do* understand," Eon said with a smile.

Lotus just shook his head in exasperation. Although he did understand in a sense, he just didn't care much for his father's matter-of-fact approach to the subject.

"By the way," Eon continued, "you'll be pleased to hear that the ship my sister sent to attack your people did relatively little damage before we captured it."

A look of shock came across Lotus' face. "What?! What ship?"

"I thought you knew. She sent a battleship to human-occupied space with orders to attack — probably an object lesson for you for defying her in some way."

"Possibly," Lotus agreed, "but she stated to me her intention to eventually enslave humanity. Maybe this was just a way to test our defenses and see how much of a fight we'd put up. Regardless, I'm grateful for your help."

"Of course, my son. I will be here whenever you need me. However, please remember that you will rule here one day in my stead, so at some juncture you will have to return and learn to govern."

"So you've said, but I'm not ready yet."

"Understood, but bear in mind that I can't wait indefinitely. The royal blood in our veins grants us extraordinarily long life, but none of us live forever."

"I will keep that in mind, Father."

"Very well. Until next time, take care of yourself, my son."

Eon's image began to fade, but as it did, something began tickling at the back of Lotus' brain like an itch he couldn't scratch. And then, just as his father's face faded completely, it came to him.

"Wait!" he shouted. "How do I get back to my own continuum?"

There was no verbal response, but at the far end of the conference table there was suddenly a flash of light as a dimensional rift opened. Lotus warily came to his feet, thinking he understood the situation but ready for anything in case he was wrong. Thankfully, his suspicions were proved right a moment later when Cerulean stepped through the rift just before it vanished. At least he had a ride home now.

A crackling in his ear drew Lotus' attention, as the earpiece broadcast something like static for a few seconds.

"What happened?" asked the computer. "For a brief period I lost all contact with you, although my self-diagnostic could discern no operational errors."

"I had a visitor who's a little shy," Lotus replied. "He likes to remain anonymous."

"I take it you are not referring to the Enforcer now in the room with you."

"Ahhhh…no." Lotus gestured towards the colossus at the other end of the table. "Computer, meet Cerulean. Cerulean, this is—"

"If you don't mind," said the computer, interrupting, "I have actually settled on a name for myself."

"Really?" Lotus remarked, raising an eyebrow. "Well, let's hear it."

"I think I like…Cherie."

"Very well, then," Lotus said, laughing, and then continued with the introductions. "Cerulean, meet my good friend, Cherie."

THE END

*Ian Lotus will return in *Chronos Ring #3*

Thank you for purchasing this book! If you enjoyed it, please feel free to leave a review on the site from which it was purchased.

Also, if you would like to be notified when I release new books, please subscribe to my mailing list via the following link: http://eepurl.com/b0-hBL

Finally, for those who may be interested, I have included my blog info: http://earlehardman.blogspot.com/

Made in United States
Orlando, FL
27 March 2024